To Lauren Carlton, Carlos Diaz, and Angelica Polis, I dedicate this to you three for your hard work because without you, this would not have been possible. This story started in 2018 only to slowly evolve into what you see before you. The story is based on separate dreams that I had for over the last five years. A lot of thought, love, and care went into this story.

I also dedicate this to you, my dear reader!

Prologue

Someone once said every city is the same. Chicago is no exception; it's dark, grimy, and in winter, it becomes extremely cold. The winters here are unforgiving, and the previous winter showed me the full force of its fury. While people often wish for snow on Christmas Eve, my wish that year was to propose to my girlfriend of four years, Claire. I know it may sound cliché, but I had every reason to do so.

Christmas Eve proposals have been a cherished tradition in the Knox family for five generations. Claire had no inkling of my plan. It was a day and a moment that would forever be etched in my memory.

Have You Seen Me? My Name is Claire Hines

Chapter 1

Valentine's Night

I still vividly remember the moment I proposed to her. That Christmas Eve remains a cherished memory for both of us. This year, Valentine's Day happened to fall on a Saturday. Despite the gentle snowfall, we decided to venture out and attend a play called "My Lover's Rose." It depicted a poignant love story, where the protagonist tragically loses his wife. The mere thought of losing Claire was enough to break my heart.

Now seems like an opportune moment to share how our paths first crossed. Ours wasn't a typical meeting through the internet or at a bar like most people experience. No, our connection began through her sister, Amanda. I've known Amanda for six years since we met in a psychology class at Duke University, and we've remained close friends ever since. It was a year later when Amanda introduced me to Claire, and we instantly clicked.

Sadly, Claire had lost both her parents in a car

accident before we had the chance to meet. Amanda is now her sole family.

Having read the positive reviews, we had eagerly anticipated the play for quite some time.

Claire's breath formed delicate clouds in the frigid February night.

"It's bitterly cold tonight, Michael."

I smiled, not because of the cold, but because of how she said it. Her green eyes mirrored the glistening snowflakes. Her fiery, flowing red hair swayed gently in the wintry breeze. Her fair complexion was shielded by warm garments. I reached out and clasped her gloved hand. "I'm glad we're here. You've always had a romantic spirit." I chuckled, "Let's find our seats and settle in. The play is about to begin."

The welcoming warmth of the Steppenwolf Theater enveloped us as we took our seats. The ambiance felt intimate and personal. Once the play commenced, I became captivated. Claire leaned forward in her chair, completely engrossed in both the performances and the

Have You Seen Me? My Name is Claire Hines

5

lyrics. Their love story was a true reflection of ours. The actors' gaze mirrored the romantic intensity of our own. Throughout the entire play, her hand clung to mine. The husband in the story did his utmost to shield his wife from a fatal car accident, but tragically, she perished. His heart was forever changed thereafter. The play's conclusion left us emotionally stunned. As we stepped out of the theater, we held each other's hands a little tighter.

The sound of snow crunching beneath our shoes reverberated through the empty street. Despite our attempt to dress appropriately for the night, we had forgotten our winter boots. The numbness from the freezing temperatures made me regret prioritizing style over practicality. We interlocked our arms tightly as we continued along the deserted sidewalk. A biting, gusty wind wrapped around us.

"I think we should call an Uber or a cab, Michael. What do you think?" Claire suggested.

"Yeah, it's getting late, and I doubt the bus will come," I agreed.

Have You Seen Me? My Name is Claire Hines

I reached into my pocket and retrieved my phone, only to see a disheartening 10% battery remaining symbol. The unsettling realization of my dying phone made me clench my teeth. *Why hadn't I charged it earlier?*

"Okay, it's done. I managed to book us a ride, but they won't be here for another seven minutes," I reluctantly informed Claire. "Hopefully, my phone won't die before then."

Claire looked at me and released a sigh. I sensed her unease, not solely due to the biting cold, but also because of our solitude on that desolate street.

"Nice night for a romantic stroll, isn't it?" a raspy, unfamiliar voice abruptly interrupted us.

We turned to find an unkempt elderly man standing nearby, like an unwelcome statue abandoned in the snow. The stench of stale cigarettes and whiskey emanated from him. His long brown trench coat bore stains and tears. His unforgettable face etched itself into my memory—a patchy white beard adorned his chin, and his grimace exposed broken yellow teeth. His eyes, as black as coal, were

Have You Seen Me? My Name is Claire Hines

sunken within his wrinkled eye sockets. A blue fisherman's cap adorned his head. He extended his right fingerless gloved hand, revealing a small handgun.

"I hate to ruin the moment, but I'll need you to hand over that lady's ring," he demanded. The yellow tint of his teeth reflected the artificial streetlight looming above us.

Claire cautiously removed her left glove, exposing her diamond ring. "How did you know?" she nervously inquired.

"Oh, a pretty, wealthy couple," he paused to inhale the frigid air. "I know your type. Arrogant, naive. You never even considered the consequences. All alone on this dark, desolate street in the dead of winter," he chuckled maliciously.

"Please, can't you just let us go?" Claire pleaded. I dared not reach for my phone, fearing any sudden movement might escalate the situation.

"Here, take it," Claire said with anger, handing him the ring.

Have You Seen Me? My Name is Claire Hines

"But that's not all I want," his raspy voice croaked. "No, you see, like you, I am also greedy. But first, we need to take care of a little business. I have an obstacle to remove."

"An obstacle?" I tightly gripped Claire's hand. All the days I had spent throughout my life, from schooling to the proposal, even the play we attended tonight, none of it had prepared me for this moment.

He ominously cocked the gun and sneered, "Say goodbye, Michael."

Have You Seen Me? My Name is Claire Hines

Chapter 2

Awakening

The consistent beeping sound jolted me back to reality. "All right, I'm awake already!" I flailed my arms around, searching for my alarm clock, only to realize there wasn't one. As my vision cleared, I found myself surrounded by the twinkle of random machines monitoring my heart rate, oxygen level, and other vital signs. The hospital room felt cold and empty. Apparently, I hadn't made it home after the incident. Suddenly, my thoughts fixated on Claire. *Where is Claire?*

The last thing I could recall was that villainous stranger who left me feeling like I had been struck by a semi-truck.

I attempted to sit up slowly, but a sharp pain surged through my side near my lung. It felt as though I had been stabbed with a searing blade. My hand instinctively reached for the source of the pain, encountering the fuzzy

Have You Seen Me? My Name is Claire Hines

texture of the gauze. It felt warm to the touch, yet uncomfortable.

"What the hell happened to me?" I blurted out in confusion.

"I see you're awake," a nurse named Maggie entered the room, her presence comforting. "I'll be taking care of you during your recovery."

She moved around the hospital bed, inspecting the lifeless IV bag hanging above me.

"What... what happened to me?" I managed to ask, my voice trembling from the pain pulsating through my wounds.

"Take it easy, Michael. You're still recovering from the gunshot wounds," Maggie explained gently.

"Gunshots?" I whispered, gingerly running my left hand over the protective gauze.

"Yes, you were shot twice. It's crucial not to strain yourself and risk reopening the wounds," she cautioned, her eyes focused on her notes.

I glanced at Maggie, finding solace in her presence. She reminded me of my mother, albeit younger. Her wavy

Have You Seen Me? My Name is Claire Hines

brunette hair was neatly tucked into a bun, and navy-blue scrubs adorned her tan skin. Her brown eyes held a sense of reassurance.

"Which hospital is this?" I inquired, trying to gather my bearings.

"You're at Northwestern Hospital," Maggie replied, meeting my gaze.

"And Claire? Where is she? Is she okay?" I anxiously asked, hoping for positive news.

The nurse returned to her notes and jotted something down in her notepad. "Who? Claire? I'm sorry, but I don't know anyone by that name. When you were admitted, you were alone and in critical condition. You've been unconscious for the past few days. Today is February 19th."

"Five days? Are you kidding me? I've been here for five days? What the hell happened to me?" I exclaimed, the realization hitting me like a freight train.

The nurse glanced at me. Her expression filled with empathy. "As I mentioned earlier, you arrived alone with

Have You Seen Me? My Name is Claire Hines

two gunshot wounds. It's truly remarkable that you survived and suffered no major organ damage. A passerby saw you lying on the ground, covered in blood, and immediately called 911. If it weren't for their quick action, you might not have made it. Now, get some rest. I'll have Dr. Swanson come in to speak with you. He's a caring doctor and has been concerned about you. Don't worry, you're in good hands. Rest," the nurse assured me, her touch providing a sense of reassurance.

I closed my eyes and allowed myself to drift into much-needed sleep. Despite the uncomfortable hospital bed and the constant interruptions, I knew I had to regain my strength before I could unravel what had happened to Claire.

Several hours passed, and it was during a less-than-appetizing meal of beef stroganoff that Dr. Swanson finally entered the room. The rubbery noodles and peculiar taste of the meat distracted me as I wondered about its origin. Nevertheless, my attention shifted as the doctor began to speak.

Have You Seen Me? My Name is Claire Hines

"I see you're enjoying your lunch. Do you want me to come back later?" the doctor asked as he took a seat at the foot of my bed. His appearance, with slicked-back blond hair and green eyes, seemed more like that of a Ken doll than a doctor.

With my mouth full of the unappetizing meal, I shook my head in response. The doctor smiled, seemingly amused by my struggle to speak.

"Maggie checked your vitals, and you're making great progress. You should be out of here in no time. I'd say three more weeks," he informed me.

"Three more weeks?" I managed to utter, surprised by the lengthy timeline.

The doctor chuckled, "Chew, Michael, chew. We don't want you choking now."

I took a hearty gulp and composed myself.

"Ugh, I don't know if I can last that long, doc. This food is terrible," I complained.

Have You Seen Me? My Name is Claire Hines

The doctor laughed, appreciating my sense of humor despite the ordeal I had been through. As for Claire, he explained that there was no information about her since I was found alone. However, he mentioned that a detective would be visiting me in a few days to provide further assistance. He has some questions to ask you. I will mention this woman to him.

"Is she a friend?" the doctor inquired, sensing my frustration.

I stared at the remnants of my lunch, feeling a mix of disgust and unease. The news of no one knowing who Claire was lately left me suspicious and deeply worried. The realization hit me like a plummeting elevator, dragging my heart down with it. The weight of sadness settled upon me, suffocating like a broken cord. I had to escape this place. I needed answers.

The pain from the gunshot wounds intensified, amplifying the already overwhelming anguish. I reclined, attempting to ease the jarring pain. It wasn't just physical, but the culmination of everything that had unfolded. The uncertainty surrounding Claire brewed a storm of shattered emotions and fear within the recesses of my mind.

"Michael?"

"Doctor, she's my fiancée and she's missing."

Chapter 3

Ides of March

"So, tell me what happened on February 14th, from the beginning," the detective said, flipping open his small, brown pocket notebook.

He sat in the visitor's chair facing me, fitting the stereotypical profile of a detective with his attire. Dressed in tan slacks, dark brown loafers, and a white shirt covered by a gray sport coat, he looked more like a model than a serious professional. His black spectacles sat perched on his stubby nose, and his sunken black eyes reflected the toll of his demanding job.

I began retelling the story from that fateful night, recounting recent events involving nurse Maggie and Doctor Swanson. I dove into childhood memories, mentioning my parents in Saratoga, NY, before reliving the encounter with the man who shot me. The repetition of the night's events felt exhausting and depressing, but it was necessary to provide the detective with all the details.

Have You Seen Me? My Name is Claire Hines

After finishing my account, I expressed my eagerness to find Claire. I wanted answers and felt a sense of urgency as my release from the hospital was only three days away. I asked the detective if he had any leads or information.

Frank, adjusting his glasses, returned a stern gaze. "I'm going to be perfectly honest with you, Michael. We thoroughly searched the area and found no evidence of your fiancée. There was no trace of her hair or blood at the crime scene. Once you're discharged, come to the precinct. We can have you meet our sketch artist, Rodrigo. Don't worry, we will catch this guy."

Frank stood up and handed me his business card, assuring me that Claire's absence of evidence indicated she might not be harmed. Though not reassuring enough, it was something to hold on to. After Frank left, I decided to make another attempt to contact Amanda, Claire's sister.

Dialing Amanda's number, I left my fourth message, pleading for her to return my call as soon as possible. The uncertainty of not knowing Claire's whereabouts weighed heavily on me. I dimmed my phone and turned my gaze toward the hospital window, finding solace in the beautiful view despite the winter's grip still lingering.

Three weeks later, as I stepped outside the hospital, the bittersweet feeling of leaving mixed with the winter temperatures. The crunch of snow under my feet reminded me of the night I was shot. Mrs. Volinsky, the building manager, greeted me outside the apartment complex, bundled up in her magenta snowsuit.

She expressed concern about my absence and insisted I come over for a meal. Though the pain at my side protested, I accepted her kind offer. Entering my apartment, the emptiness engulfed me, emphasizing Claire's absence. I settled in, made a cup of tea, and sorted through the mail, finding mostly advertising and get-well cards.

In need of information, I called Frank, who informed me of a body matching Claire's description found at the trainyard in Pilsen. Without uttering a word, I hung up and

Have You Seen Me? My Name is Claire Hines

hurried to the location. The air felt dense and numbing, adding to the sinking feeling of dread in my stomach. Frank awaited me at the top of the icy ramp, his brown trench coat dancing in the wind.

Preparing myself for the worst, I took a deep breath and followed Frank toward the crime scene. Police officers and medical personnel surrounded the area, some jotting down notes, while others set up yellow police tape. One officer interviewed a shaken passerby who had discovered the body.

Bracing myself, I mentally prepared for what lay ahead. The sound of crunching snow grew louder as we approached the scene, and I steeled myself with a calming breath. Several police officers and medical personnel gathered around, their presence a somber indication of the seriousness of the situation.

Chapter 4

The Body

The pungent odor of rotting flesh and spoiled blood was never a scent I wanted to experience. I remember going to the butcher shop in a Ukrainian Village with my mother when I was a child to purchase various meats, she'd cook for Sunday dinner. Why she decided to cook such strange dishes on a Sunday baffled me as a child, but that childhood memory of the scent of an animal's corpse never faded. This memory is where my mind currently lingers.

I suppose it's my brain's way of trying to prepare me of what will be revealed beneath the white, bloodstained blanket draped over this woman's corpse. The medical examiner slowly revealed the woman's face that left me preparing for the worst. But luckily it wasn't her and instead, a combination relief and anguish escaped my lungs.

I felt pity for the woman, but at least this wasn't Claire.

Have You Seen Me? My Name is Claire Hines

"Well, is it her?" Frank questioned me with a respectful whisper, as if we were in a library or study hall.

I looked at Frank and shook my head, "No, it's not her. I don't know who this woman is, but whoever did this…"

"I know Michael. Whoever did this is a real sick individual."

The nameless corpse, or what was left of it, lied in large pool of dried and frozen blood. Snow and debris covered some of the woman's limbs, which were in pieces and decapitated from her body.

"Sir, we found something!" one of the medical examiners shouted.

Frank peered toward the medical examiner, who knelt near the decapitated head of the woman.

"I found something inside this woman's mouth. Let me extract it."

"Be careful, Kalinksi," warned Frank.

"It has a name on it." Kalinski paused and examined the note with his blue latex gloves. "It's addressed to … Michael?" He looked at me with confusion.

Have You Seen Me? My Name is Claire Hines

"Me? Why would anyone leave a note like this inside?" I stopped speaking because I couldn't finish my sentence. This experience weighed heavily on me and I wanted no part of it. I wished to be back inside my apartment with Claire. I yearned for my life to return to the way it was before this all happened.

I wanted her back.

"Check for prints then let me see what it says," Frank said. He placed his hands into latex examination gloves. Another one of the detectives checked the note for fingerprints and scrunched his aging forehead. Frank looked at me. "Are you sure you don't recognize this woman?"

I nodded in affirmation. I wanted to say something, but the words escaped me. The shock of a note addressed to me that was found within this nameless woman's decapitated head left me startled and perplexed.

What… what kind of sick monster would do this? I whispered under my breath.

Have You Seen Me? My Name is Claire Hines

"Nothing found sir, no prints, it's clean." The medical examiner handed Frank the note.

Frank turned to me, "Let's go back to my office and we'll take a look at the note. Maybe it'll give some clues to what's going on."

I quickly nodded. I would give anything to leave this dreadful scene. The image of this poor woman will haunt my memories and dreams for weeks.

Frank's Office

After I settled into the leather office chair, my body still felt uncomfortable and tense. It wasn't from the cold outside, but from what was contained within the depths of that note, as it innocently rested at the center of Frank's desk. It reminded me of a love note passed around during a class in high school.

"Here take some of this, it'll warm you up. My mother used to give me this whenever I needed a little relaxation," Frank said while handing me a Styrofoam cup. "Careful, it's hot."

Have You Seen Me? My Name is Claire Hines

I smiled nervously and took the cup. The warm sweet

scent of the chamomile tea filled my nose.

"I hope you don't mind, Michael…"

"Oh, I like honey," I said without letting Frank finish his

sentence.

He chuckled, "No, I mean, I hope you don't mind if I look at

the note first. I want to comb through it for any evidence or

leads first since I'll read it with a clear mind."

I nodded in embarrassment.

"Sure, I don't mind."

The sweet liquid wrapped around my tongue as I

watched Frank's expression turn sour as he read the note.

He rested his hand beneath his fat chin while his eyebrows

curled, and his bottom lip folded over the top one. Finally,

what felt more like hours than a few minutes, he returned

his gaze to me. "Here, you better take a look at this."

I nervously extended my right arm and grasped the

thin folded paper. My hand shook slightly as I unfolded it.

My eyes rapidly bounced between every word:

Have You Seen Me? My Name is Claire Hines

Michael,

If you are reading this, then it means you found the first clue. I am sure after spending time with the cops today you had to wait to finally read this. I am sure Frank wanted a first crack at this in hopes of deciphering this note. I must apologize to you. I know you were expecting to find someone else, but I wanted to give you a taste of my art. What did you think?

Now let's get to the meat of this shall we? Meat, that's all humans are, a bag of meat. In case you are wondering, yes, she is safe.

But where is she? And why did I hide this note in the mouth of my first victim. The answer lies in the second victim.

Let's begin, shall we?

Solve this riddle and you will find the next clue,

But if you take too long you will end up a fool.

She will not last long, hurry to her aid,

Right now, her life is beginning to fade.

She is in a place beneath the living ghosts,

Have You Seen Me? My Name is Claire Hines

Her body hangs, but slowly she roasts.

But please be quick, for the candle is losing its wick.

Like a baseball player you play a game, but this one is not the same.

Bases loaded will you strike out or hit a home run,

Better go now before the third setting sun.

After reading the note I folded it and looked at Frank.

"So now what?" I felt hopeless after reading it. A game? What kind of sick person is this? Why would they treat someone's life like a game?"

Frank cleared his throat and sat in his leather chair. "We're going to need some help on this. This is over our heads and my paygrade. It's time I call in the cavalry. Go home and get some rest, we'll start figuring this out tomorrow morning.

Have You Seen Me? My Name is Claire Hines

Chapter 5

Victim Two

"Her name is Rita. She worked as a bartender at the diner on Lincoln Avenue. Her boss reported that she has been missing since last Sunday," Frank said, rubbing his chubby face.

"The last person who saw her that night was her manager. He said she left alone, and that was the last time we saw her," he continued.

"Any witnesses?" asked the FBI agent, a hardened veteran with slicked-back brown hair, aged wrinkles on his white skin, and scars from sleepless nights of solving cases. Frank looked at him across the meeting table.

"I told you, Muller, we are reviewing surveillance, but so far nothing," Frank replied.

Muller tilted his head, and both FBI agents, dressed in their signature blue jackets with bright yellow "FBI" letters on the back, focused their attention on him.

Have You Seen Me? My Name is Claire Hines

"What do you think, Crosby?" Frank inquired.

Crosby, a mid-thirties African American woman with curly black hair and a slender build, toyed with her half-chipped red fingernail paint under the artificial fluorescent office light.

She curled her lip and spoke, "From what Frank said, it sounds like she never made it home. Someone must have been following her."

I unintentionally blurted out, "The man who shot me. It must have been him!" My sudden outburst caught the attention of both FBI agents and Frank, while the others in the room continued their low chatter.

"The man who shot you?" Crosby asked, leaning forward. I sat in the "head" chair, feeling like a magnet in the room.

Whenever I spoke or made a gesture, Crosby noticed. I wondered if she was suspicious of me or if I was the one behind this crime.

Have You Seen Me? My Name is Claire Hines

"Yeah, if it's the same guy who kidnapped Claire, then he could have easily kidnapped this woman by grabbing her while she was distracted," I explained.

"You seem to know a lot about how the killer thinks," Crosby declared, narrowing her eyes. It seemed as if she suspected me of having a hidden motive or being involved in the crime.

"No, I'm only suspecting this because of what happened to me. We were approached by this man, and all I'm saying is—"

"What you're saying is completely hypothetical, but not that far-fetched," interrupted Muller.

"Let's go over that riddle again," Crosby suggested, suddenly smiling calmly at me. Perhaps I had misjudged her, and she didn't suspect me at all. Maybe this was her way of being professional and cordial with me.

"What about the riddle? We have to solve this, or else we'll have another death on our hands," Frank said, impatiently tapping his pen on his notepad.

Have You Seen Me? My Name is Claire Hines

Crosby clasped her hands together. "We know there's a baseball reference. Could it refer to one of our local teams? The Cubs or the Sox? Maybe she's at one of the stadiums."

"Muller," I interjected, "It might be a line in there to throw us off, too. The killer made a few references to fire. Look," I placed my finger on several lines and read them aloud. "Her body hangs, but slowly she roasts. But please be quick, for the candle is losing its wick." I looked up, envisioning Claire as the woman hanging over a fire.

"That's it!" I exclaimed. "This woman is hanging over a pit of fire."

"If that's the case, wouldn't she already be dead?" Muller frowned. "She might already be dead."

"Now, let's not give up hope! She could be hanging by a rope, and something is slowly cutting that rope away," I suggested.

Chapter 6

Twins

"I have an idea of where we need to go!" I exclaimed as
Crosby and I entered Frank's office. Frank and Muller were
seated across from each other, sharing Frank's large oak
desk, which was covered with scattered papers and small,
empty Chinese takeout containers from lunch.

"Michael, calm down," Frank said calmly, motioning for me
to take a seat beside Muller, who turned his head to look at
me.

"What did you find out?" Muller asked with a smug tone.

I couldn't quite put my finger on it, but there was
something about Muller that rubbed me the wrong way.
Maybe it was his condescending demeanor or his choice of
words, but I found it difficult to work with him on this case.

"Michael is correct," Crosby interrupted. "We would need to
do more investigation, but we believe we have a lead."

Have You Seen Me? My Name is Claire Hines

"And what exactly would that be?" Muller asked, his tone filled with intrigue.

"We think the victim is being held at the power plant located on the Southside of the city. It would make sense since it was powered by coal," Crosby explained. "Considering the location where we found the first victim's body, we believe the next victim might be held there."

"What makes you so sure?" Muller questioned sarcastically. "Is this just a hunch? Do you have any solid proof?"

I looked at Crosby, who remained silent. "We're going off a hunch, but it feels like a strong lead," I said.

Muller chuckled. "This is why you're wrong. Both power plants in Chicago are inactive, right Frank?"

Frank cleared his throat. "Well, yes, they are inactive. But it could still make sense."

"Could make sense? Are you out of your minds? Why would the killer's next victim be at an inactive power plant?" Muller scoffed.

Have You Seen Me? My Name is Claire Hines

"Well..." Frank began to speak but seemed hesitant in the face of Muller's reaction.

"Look," I interjected. "Let's go over the poem again. He mentioned fire and made a reference to baseball."

"Baseball?" Muller scoffed. "What the hell does baseball have to do with any of this?"

"What are the names of the stations, Frank? Do you know?" I looked at Frank, hoping for some reassurance. Muller's reactions were starting to discourage me.

"Let me ask Chuck," Frank said. "His uncle used to work at the plant on the Southside." Frank stood up and left his office.

An uncomfortable silence filled the room. Crosby tapped away on her iPhone, while Muller stared out through the large office window. The view wasn't anything spectacular, just the usual urban decay. The police station was situated in a less glamorous area of Chicago, known for its crime involving drug dealers and gangbangers.

"I can't wait to get out of this crap hole," Muller declared, spinning his chair around to face us. Crosby looked up from her phone. "Seriously, Muller? We need to focus here. I asked my dad about any information he had on the power plants. He mentioned one called the Crawford station, but he wasn't sure about the other one."

"Crawford," I said aloud, but it was meant for my own thoughts. Could the second victim be there? I couldn't help but wonder if it was Claire.

Frank returned to his office and said, "Fisk. It's called the Fisk station."

Muller rubbed his chin. "Okay, this is starting to make sense now."

"It is?" I asked, surprised to hear Muller siding with us.

"Yeah," he answered. "Fisk was also the name of that baseball player, right, Frank?"

Frank cleared his throat as he sat back down at his desk. "Yeah, he played for the Sox, I think."

Have You Seen Me? My Name is Claire Hines

"Okay, this is starting to make sense since the poem made a baseball reference. So, she must be at the Fisk station!" I proclaimed.

"Now hold on just a minute, cowboy," Muller advised, waving his index finger at me. "Let's be rational about this."

"What's there to be rational about?" I asked impatiently.

Muller frowned at my argumentative tone. "If this guy is smart and cunning, which it seems he is, then this could be a clever ruse."

As much as I wanted to disagree, Muller had a valid point.

"This could be a trap. If she really is at Fisk, then why would it be easy to solve this riddle? Answer me that," Muller said.

"He's right, Michael," Crosby added, resting her hand on my lap. "Let's be logical. We need to be patient and approach this tactfully. I understand you want to find Claire, but we have to be realistic."

"Could the victim be at the other power plant? Maybe we should send two teams to each one."

Have You Seen Me? My Name is Claire Hines

Frank's suggestion made sense. It wouldn't hurt to investigate both locations.

Muller toyed with his blue pen. "Okay, I'll bite. Let's send two teams to each location. I'll lead the first team to Fisk. If she's there, I'll radio you to call off your search at the other location, Crosby."

Crosby nodded in agreement.

"Muller, Crosby," Frank said sternly. "I will assign three officers to each of you. I'll go with Muller. Michael, I want you to stay put. Crosby, I'll assign a team to you. Muller, can she handle going on her own?"

"Now wait a minute," I interjected. "I want to be there with Crosby. What if the woman being held is Claire? I need to be there. I promise not to get in the way, really."

Frank looked at Crosby, who remained silent.

"Alright, it's fine. He can go with me. It was his hunch after all," Crosby said, looking at me with a smile.

I returned the smile and noticed Muller wearing a sour expression.

Have You Seen Me? My Name is Claire Hines

"I don't like it, but it makes sense. I don't want Crosby going in alone. But you better stay out of her way, Michael," Muller declared sharply.

It felt like he was acting as my father or a stern teacher. I didn't like it, but I didn't want to argue. They trusted me to go with Crosby, and I didn't want to ruin my chances of being there.

"I won't get in anyone's way. Trust me!"

Chapter 7

Pregame

I watched as both tactical teams geared up, feeling a sense of satisfaction that we were finally making progress. It was also reassuring that they had included me in this excursion.

"Michael," Crosby said, adjusting her bulletproof vest. "Do you have experience with firearms?"

She asked me while I adjusted the vest on my shoulders, feeling its snug and heavy weight.

"Yeah, sort of. My dad used to take me hunting in Indiana when I was a kid. Back then, though, I used a Remington rifle," I replied.

Crosby handed me a handgun and said, "I don't expect you to have to use this, but it's just a precaution."

I nodded and gripped the cold handle, which felt more like a hammer than a handgun.

Have You Seen Me? My Name is Claire Hines

After we finished gearing up, we entered a large loading dock where two separate black vans were waiting for us. Muller and his team, dressed in black tactical gear with covered faces and stowed weapons, stood nearby.

"Listen up!" Muller shouted as he secured his weapon. "

"We're going in nice and quiet. It'll be Frank and me, plus three officers. This will be a smooth operation. We're heading to the Fisk power plant. Crosby and Michael will lead three officers into the Crawford station. I don't know what to expect or if we'll find anything there, but this needs to be done by the books. I don't want any funny business. Our call sign is Foxhound. Crosby, your team's call sign is Foxhole."

"You want Michael to go in there with us?" Crosby asked, clipping her handgun.

"If his fiancée is in there, we need him to be there to identify her," Muller replied.

"And what if she's not? You're putting him at risk. He is a liabil—"

Have You Seen Me? My Name is Claire Hines

"Look," Muller interrupted, turning his gaze towards me. "You will follow my orders. He can handle himself, right?"

Muller's cold, serious stare felt like a dagger piercing me, but I maintained my composure and replied, "Yeah, I got this, don't worry. I can hold my own."

I holstered my borrowed hardware, feeling its weight and the false sense of protection it provided. I knew I was in over my head, but I couldn't show it. Claire's safety was paramount, and I couldn't afford to fail her.

"All right, people! Let's load up and move out!" Muller shouted, waving his arm and directing his team into the black, discreet police van.

He looked at us and nodded, resembling a proud father watching his children start their first day of college. "You two watch yourselves out there. Let's get back in one piece!"

Crosby and I exchanged a nod, silently acknowledging the gravity of the situation. I wanted to assure her that we would be fine, but deep down, I knew

Have You Seen Me? My Name is Claire Hines

the reality of our predicament. It was my first time in the field, and she knew it too.

I took a seat in the dark van beside two unnamed officers, feeling the discomfort of the cold and uncomfortable bench. The tinted windows blocked out the sunlight, creating a stuffy and hot environment. No one said anything, and the tension inside the van was palpable. We all knew this operation would determine whether we made it out alive.

I glanced at Crosby and exhaled nervously. Our eyes met through our masks, and though I wanted to engage in small talk, the presence of the other officers kept me silent.

"ETA fifteen minutes, get ready!" the officer driving the van yelled. Rain suddenly clattered against the roof, and the lights stayed off to maintain a low profile. In this unpredictable weather, our presence would likely go unnoticed in the vacant streets.

The streetlights reflected off the puddles and heavy rain as I stepped out of the vehicle. It felt cold and dreary, making me yearn for my bed and the warm touch of Claire.

I sighed beneath my tactical mask, which fogged up not

from my breath, but from the cold rain pelting against it.

"Let's move. Michael, stay close behind. Naminski will

cover us," Crosby said, her voice muffled by the mask.

Thunder lightly rumbled in the background.

"Roger that, Crosby," Naminski replied. Wearing the gear

was uncomfortable, but I understood its purpose – to keep

me alive.

"Parker, open the gate slowly and check for any traps."

"Copy that, Crosby."

Through the mix of falling rain and thunder, I faintly

heard the whining of the steel gate as it opened.

"Looks clear. Move in," ordered Parker as he took point.

With the power off, there were no lights within the

Crawford power plant. It appeared abandoned and eerie,

and lightning flashes against the long stained industrial

windows gave the impression that somebody or something

was watching our approach.

"Door is unsecured. Going in slowly," Parker reported.

Have You Seen Me? My Name is Claire Hines

I leaned against the slick brick wall, feeling the beads of water rattle against my body as I crouched. Thunder clashed above us as the rain continued to fall.

"Looks clear," declared Parker.

"Copy that," replied Crosby, placing her hand on my shoulder. "Let's move in, people. Follow my lead. Michael, stay close."

"I will," I answered, trying to sound confident despite the unease within me.

The concrete floor inside the power plant was dry, with occasional drips of water from the deteriorating roof. Rainfall violently rattled against the windows and the remaining parts of the thin metal roof.

We crept forward, our flashlights guiding us through the darkness.

"Watch out for these pipes," Parker advised as he moved ahead.

"The less noise we make, the better. We don't know who's here with us," added Crosby.

"I found a service entrance to the basement," said Parker, opening the large metal door stealthily. Despite its size, it made minimal noise.

We descended a few flights of stairs to enter the basement, greeted by a large, dark tunnel connecting the main floor to the basement. The air felt damp and cold as we made our way inside, with echoes of conversations between sewer rats and our footsteps reverberating against the tunnel walls.

It was difficult to remain silent in the tunnel, as our presence was easily detected by the acoustics. If someone was waiting for us, they would already know we were here. "I located the entrance to the basement. The door is locked. I'm going to need a hand prying this thing open," Parker said.

"Naminski, help Parker. I'll cover you," Crosby ordered.

"Roger that, Crosby. Moving to you, Parker," replied Naminski.

"Affirmative. We'll have to use the shotgun. I don't see any room for a crowbar."

Have You Seen Me? My Name is Claire Hines

"I don't like this," Crosby expressed her concern. "If someone is waiting for us, they will definitely hear the gunfire."

"There's no other way. It's either the shotgun or the C4. Unfortunately, we can't use the C4 here since it could cause a collapse. Plus, none of us would want to go deaf from the explosion. It's too risky."

"Alright, Parker. You made your point," Crosby conceded.

Though I wanted to contribute to their conversation, I decided it was best to remain silent. The height and shape of the tunnel made me feel uneasy, despite not being claustrophobic. The pitch-black darkness only heightened my discomfort, and if it weren't for our flashlights, we would be engulfed in total darkness.

The loud shots from the shotgun shattered the silence, jolting my body awkwardly from the two loud booms. My ears rang slightly from the gunfire.

"Well, that was loud enough to wake the dead," Naminski attempted to lighten the situation.

Have You Seen Me? My Name is Claire Hines

Another loud clang echoed through the tunnel as the heavy metal door fell against the concrete floor.

"If someone was waiting for us, they definitely know we're here," Parker stated.

"Stay alert. Let's move in," Crosby urged, determined to keep her team focused.

"Roger that," Parker responded. "I'll take point."

This was it. Whether I was ready or not, it was time to enter the basement.

Chapter 8

The Basement

The basement was cold, damp, and shrouded in darkness, save for the feeble beams of our flashlights. The sound of dripping water echoed sporadically, coming from various unknown sources. I wondered if it was rainwater or something more sinister.

The putrid stench that filled the air was a horrid blend of sewer odor and decayed animals. I couldn't decide which was worse: navigating through the darkness in this nauseating smell or the fear of what we might stumble upon.

Even though I breathed through my mouth, the unpleasant odor still invaded my senses. My flashlight flickered slightly as I held it in front of me.

"I think my batteries are starting to die," I remarked.

"Nah, mine too. It's probably due to electrical interference down here. Did any of you notice?" Parker paused. "But we've been going deeper."

The path we walked on was not only narrow but also inclined. In the dim light, I spotted unfamiliar heavy machinery, likely responsible for powering the plant.

"This is where they used to store coal and operate large furnaces. Watch your step," Naminski informed us.

"How the hell do you know that, Naminski?" Parker asked.

"My dad used to work at this power plant," he replied.

"Is that why it stinks? Where's the smell coming from?" I questioned.

"I'm not sure. There are big sewer rats down here with red eyes. Be careful; they have a nasty bite."

Great, now I had rats to worry about too.

"Enough chitchat. Let's focus on finding what we came for," ordered Crosby, her voice tinged with anxiety. She clearly disliked being down here as much as the rest of us.

"I see something up ahead! I'm going to check it out. Hold on, team," Parker exclaimed, his voice filled with excitement.

"Parker, be careful and don't do anything stupid. Naminski, cover him. Michael and I will stay behind."

I wanted to go with them in case they found her. If they did, I would have to identify the body.

"Strange, we found a small wooden chest on the ground here. We need more light down here," Parker called out.

We followed them down the incline, our flashlights painting their bodies' silhouettes in the darkness. They seemed like eerie spirits waiting for us, sending a shiver down my spine.

"What do we have here? Treasure?" I jokingly asked.

"We don't know what it is! Don't try to move it; it could be a bomb," Crosby warned.

"Chill, Crosby," said Parker. "I got this."

He pulled out a lockpick and skillfully worked on the large lock securing the chest. After a few minutes, Parker successfully opened it.

"Open it slowly," cautioned Crosby.

"I've got it, Crosby. Wow, this is weird."

"What do you see, Parker?"

"There's a letter inside. It's addressed to Michael."

"Me? What?" I asked, surprised but somehow expecting it.

Whoever left the letter here knew I would be here.

"Here, this is for you. Open it," said Parker, handing me the envelope.

With trembling hands, I struggled to open the envelope. Despite the strong beam of my flashlight, I managed to read the contents.

"It's another riddle," I announced.

"What does it say, Michael?" Crosby inquired.

"Let me read it to you."

You have made it this far

The other station is now brighter than a star

Venture forward because time is on a wire

The others will burn from the fire

"Okay, this riddle makes no sense. What the hell does it mean, Crosby?" I asked, a sense of foreboding washing over me.

Have You Seen Me? My Name is Claire Hines

"Ugh, I can't get a signal down here. Can anyone hear me?" Crosby yelled into her walkie-talkie, frustration evident in her voice.

"What's wrong, Crosby?" Parker asked.

"Muller's team is at the other station, and I can't reach them. I think they're in trouble. Parker, take Michael and keep going. I'm going back to the surface to contact the other team."

"Got it, boss," Parker confirmed.

"Are you sure about this?" I questioned Crosby.

"Yeah, just stay close to Parker. It'll be the three of you. I'll be fine."

"Got it," Naminski replied.

"Stay close to us, Michael. We've got your back," assured Parker. He illuminated his shotgun with his flashlight, piercing through the pitch-black darkness.

I didn't feel entirely comfortable staying behind with Naminski and Parker. Both officers seemed to approach the situation with a cocky attitude.

Have You Seen Me? My Name is Claire Hines

As we ventured deeper into the dark tunnel, I glanced back several times, watching Crosby's flashlight gradually fade into darkness. Soon after, we reached the end of the tunnel.

"There's another steel door, but someone left it open," Naminski observed distractedly.

"Parker, stay here," he ordered.

Officer Naminski proceeded inside, leaving Parker and me standing in the dark tunnel.

"It looks like it's just you and me, buddy," Parker remarked.

Even in the darkness, I could sense his arrogance and smugness. He didn't take the situation seriously, which bothered me. I wanted to protest, but now wasn't the time for a fight.

After what felt like an eternity of silence, we heard Naminski's voice coming through the walkie-talkie.

"Should we try contacting Naminski, Parker?" I suggested.

Parker adjusted his tactical helmet and shook his head.

Have You Seen Me? My Name is Claire Hines

"My flashlight is starting to dim again. This battery has maybe thirty more minutes left before it dies out," I said.

"Here, Michael, take mine. The battery is stronger. Give me your flashlight, and stay here. I'll go see where Naminski went."

"Naminski, come in. Do you read us?" I called into the walkie-talkie. Moments of silence passed until the sound of crackling static jolted me.

"I—ca—nooooo!" Naminski's voice crackled through the other end. "He—" His voice abruptly ended, followed by continuous static.

"Come in. Repeat what you said, Naminski. Do you read me?"

"Crap. I have to go and check this out. Look, Michael, stay here. I don't know what the hell is going on. If I'm not back in fifteen minutes, get out of here."

"Parker—" But before I could continue, he rushed after Naminski.

Great, he left me alone here in this dark tunnel with only a flashlight, a gun, and a prayer. Uncertainty loomed over me as I wondered how long the flashlight's battery would last. It would take me some time to find my way back and exit the basement. Trying to recall the schematics,

I realized that, with tensions running high, everything felt like a maze. The basement's poor lighting made it even more challenging, and it would likely take hours to navigate my way back.

Leaning against the curved tunnel wall, I couldn't help but recall a time when Claire and I went on a camping trip. Our car had broken down on a dark Michigan highway. Although the moon provided some illumination, it was nothing compared to the pitch-black darkness surrounding me now. We had felt scared but safe together inside our Volvo. Oh, how I wished I could go back to that moment.

I switched off my flashlight and waited for thirty minutes. Despite my reluctance, going back seemed difficult. As hesitant as I was, I knew I had to go after them.

Have You Seen Me? My Name is Claire Hines

Chapter 9

Alone in the Dark

"Come in, Parker. Naminski, do you read me?" I repeated my attempts to reach them for several minutes, but all I received was static. The darkness engulfed me as I cautiously entered the open doorway, using my hand as a guide and conserving my flashlight's battery.

Inside the large room, water flooded the area, reaching up to my knees. The eerie shadows cast by the circular metal doors and pipes created a horror movie-like atmosphere. The water seeped through, soaking my legs despite my protective gear.

Navigating through the room, I followed the sound of a broken pipe, its steady stream creating a backdrop of rushing water. With each step, the water deepened, numbing my skin and adding to the sense of impending doom.

A snake-like eel brushed against my legs, but I recognized it as a sewer rat seeking refuge. The unholy ambiance of the place contrasted with its original purpose as a source of light and life. I pressed on, determined to find Naminski.

"Michael, is that you?" A weak voice called out.

"Naminski?" I responded, hoping for confirmation.

"Yeah... I am... here... follow my voice. It... will... lead... gaping hole... wall."

Naminski's voice, without his tactical mask, sounded frail. I waded through the water, which grew deeper, and followed his instructions. Eventually, I reached a large hole, where the water was less deep. Rats scurried around, feasting on a body—it was Naminski. The lower half of his body was submerged in a mixture of blood and wastewater.

Guilt and sorrow overwhelmed me as I whispered an apology. Suddenly, a haunting howl echoed from deeper within the sewer. The pungent odor of the environment forced me to remove my mask, as the mixture of sloshing sounds and rat squeaks filled the air.

Have You Seen Me? My Name is Claire Hines

Static interrupted the silence, and Parker's raspy voice called out through the walkie-talkie. He was in the sewer, urging me to get out. The radio went dead, leaving me petrified and filled with uncertainty. I pressed on, using my dying flashlight and following the occasional specs of light from the streets above.

The rats were biting at my ankles, seemed to warn me or satisfy their hunger. The echoes of my movements against the curved walls reminded me of the endless maze I found myself in. Eventually, I reached a service door, leading to an iron door that brought me to a maintenance closet.

Searching for a light switch, I found it just as my flashlight died. The fluorescent lights illuminated the blue-walled room, filled with equipment and scattered boxes. But the sight that awaited me was horrifying—Parker, suspended upside down, lifeless and pierced multiple times.

With gun in hand, I approached him, knowing he was beyond saving. The room revealed no evidence, only

Have You Seen Me? My Name is Claire Hines

random items. Through the exit, I emerged into a subway

tunnel, following a trail of bloody footprints left by the killer.

It was time to find out who was behind these

murders, as I followed the footsteps, determined to

confront the culprit.

Chapter 10

Midnight Train

I carefully stepped over the Blue Line rail tracks. This was the main train line that ushered riders to the main airport in Chicago called O'Hare Airport. The air felt warmer here in comparison to both the sewers and powerplant, but I was cold thanks to the bottom half of my clothes that were still wet from being in wastewater.

I wondered how much time passed from when I entered the powerplant. The rumbling of hunger within my stomach informed me it was longer than a few hours. In the distance, static from another walkie-talkie caught my attention. This radio may belong to Parker since his was missing when I found his body in the maintenance closet.

The ghastly image of his dangling body still haunted my memory. I walked over and found Parker's walkie-talkie resting at the center of the railway tracks. Suddenly, the radio came alive with an unexpected voice.

"Come in, is anyone there?"

It was Muller.

I picked up Parker's walkie-talkie and before I could respond he called out again.

"Come in, is anyone there? This is agent Muller."

The device felt slick in my hands because the back of it was covered in a strange fluid. My instincts told me it was blood.

This belonged to Parker, whoever left it here wanted me to find it.

"Come in, is anyone there?" Muller repeated his question.

"Muller? It's me Michael," I answered.

"Michael? Where the hell have you been? Why isn't anyone answering me? Where is everyone?"

"Crosby returned to the surface, Naminski and Parker are dead," I replied.

"Jesus, what the hell happened? No, wait don't touch that! What did the paper say again, the switch will light the fire? Michael listen, whatever you do, don't come he...NO! Dammit don't do that! Ahhhhhh!"

Have You Seen Me? My Name is Claire Hines

The conversation abruptly ended with a vulgar static noise. I nearly dropped the walkie-talkie from the vision of what happened to Muller and his team. *What exactly happened? What did Muller mean by, "The paper said the switch will light the fire?"*

I needed to return the surface and regroup with Crosby and her team.

"Going somewhere?"

The unexpected voice startled me. It sent an unwanted shiver down my spine. I froze in fear at the middle of the train tracks.

"Where are you going Michael?" the man repeated in a raspy and malicious sounding voice.

I wanted to turn around and see who it was, but I was afraid. With my back facing the man, I tried to speak, but instead, my words escaped me.

The train tracks came alive and rattled like an angry rattlesnake.

"Looks like my ride's here. See you soon dear Michael," the man declared.

Have You Seen Me? My Name is Claire Hines

I ignored his provocations and ran away. With the train approaching fast from behind, there was no time to see who it was. Quickly, I hopped over the train tracks and onto the abandoned platform. Since it was late, there were no other passengers waiting for the incoming train.

Moments later, the subway train howled into the deserted station. I wondered how the sewer maze led me to this forgotten blue line stop. The name of the station was colorfully graffitied over, but I was at the Belmont stop.

Above me the light fixtures flickered wildly as the train passed. Various lost pages from an unwanted newspaper danced in the leftover breeze. This Belmont station felt haunting.

I walked toward the end of the platform and saw large steel gates that blocked my exit. There were two stairwells that were also blocked with their own gates. I decided to resort to using my handgun as the key since no one else was around. The sound from the gunshot bounced off the filthy cured tiled walls. Luckily it only took

Have You Seen Me? My Name is Claire Hines

one shot to break the lock off. Another door greeted me after I walked up the stairwell. Luckily, it was unlocked.

Outside, the damp night air embraced me as I exited the subway station. The rain from earlier left behind a concert of chirping crickets under the late-night sky. Vapor escaped my mouth as a chill lingered. That voice from the tunnel still echoed in my mind.

Who was that? Was someone even there or was it my imagination? It felt all too real to be my imagination.

Without any clear evidence that someone was indeed behind me, I decided to keep the moment to myself. For now, my prerogative was clear, head back to the station and find out if Crosby was there. I had to know what happened to Muller and his team. Despite my differences with the man, I really hoped he was all right.

Have You Seen Me? My Name is Claire Hines

Chapter 11

Broken Dawn

The sun rose behind me as I stood outside the police station, my body battered and broken from the night before. It had been a long and harrowing night, leaving me with damp clothes, haunting memories, and missing comrades. The list of people I knew who were now missing was growing.

Inside the police station, officers gathered, some sipping coffee while others chatted or filled out paperwork at their desks. Commissioner Gomez, a stocky man, paced restlessly in his office, his thoughts clearly elsewhere. I approached his office with caution, wanting to convey everything that had happened in a coherent and composed manner, despite feeling overwhelmed by the events of the previous night.

"Hello," I said, interrupting Gomez's brooding. He appeared pleasantly surprised to see me.

"Michael, is it?" he asked.

Have You Seen Me? My Name is Claire Hines

"Yes, that's correct," I replied.

"Nice to meet you," he said, shaking my hand. "We need to talk. Please, have a seat."

Taking a seat in front of his desk, I couldn't help but notice the certificates, awards, and plaques adorning the wall behind him. The first thing on Gomez's mind was the whereabouts of Naminski and Parker.

"Where the hell are Naminski and Parker?" he asked directly, his voice commanding.

I sighed and fixed my gaze on the center of his desk, feeling a wave of unwanted guilt wash over me.

"They're... they're gone, sir," I somberly answered.

"Gone? How, Michael?" he inquired.

"I don't know how it happened, but someone killed them," I replied, my voice heavy with sadness.

Commissioner Gomez leaned back in his black leather chair, rubbing his face in frustration. I remained silent as he processed the information, my heart sinking deeper with every passing moment.

Have You Seen Me? My Name is Claire Hines

"Who killed them? Was it you?" he asked sternly, accusingly.

I was taken aback by the sudden accusation. "No! It wasn't me, sir. I was left alone in the sewer while they went to investigate a sound," I explained, my voice betraying my nervousness.

His face contorted with a mix of dislike and disappointment, as if he blamed me for their deaths and the disappearance of his team. The urge to reveal everything I had witnessed was strong, but I stayed silent, opting instead to recount the events that unfolded. I spoke of Crosby abandoning us in the basement, the fate that befell Parker and Naminski in the sewer, the cryptic conversation with Muller, and finally finding my way to the Belmont Blue Line train station.

"So, that's everything?" Gomez asked, his frustration evident as he rubbed his eyes. "I apologize for my initial reaction and questions. It's just... they're dead. All of them. Well, not all of them," he corrected himself. "Agent Crosby is missing."

Have You Seen Me? My Name is Claire Hines

"She's missing?" I asked, a glimmer of hope in my voice. Gomez sighed. "Yes. Crosby called me, stating that she was returning to the surface alone, without you and the two officers. Meanwhile, Muller's team reached the Fisk station and encountered a trap. They were caught in the furnace, surrounded by oil drums. It seems this happened while you were speaking to Muller. Someone triggered a trap that resulted in a massive explosion. It not only wiped out his team but also caused significant destruction spanning four city blocks. Michael, we lost many good people last night. I apologize for my behavior."

My heart dropped at the realization that everyone, including Frank and Muller, was gone.

"How do you know Crosby is missing?" I asked, seeking clarification.

"We found the bodies of Naminski and Parker inside the Crawford station, but Crosby's body was not among them. This gives us hope that she might still be alive," Gomez declared, walking over to the office window and staring at the rising sun.

Have You Seen Me? My Name is Claire Hines

"Their bodies were in the Crawford station?" I asked, puzzled.

"Yes," he replied.

"When I found Naminski, he was in a maintenance closet in the sewers. Someone must have moved them then."

Gomez instructed me to go home and rest, promising to update me if he heard anything. Although his voice felt cold and emotionless, I understood the weight of the situation. I sighed in defeat, willing to comply.

"Okay, I'll go home. You're right," I replied, hoping to lighten the mood.

Gomez continued to gaze out the window, his back turned to me. "Call me if you remember anything."

"Okay. Call me if you hear anything as well."

Leaving his office, I exited the station and returned to my apartment. Tossing my keys on the table, I changed out of my smelly clothes. The room was dimly lit, with the afternoon sunlight seeping through cracks in the drawn drapes.

Have You Seen Me? My Name is Claire Hines

On the table, I found a note from Mrs. Volinsky, inviting me to join her and her husband for dinner. Their unwavering support over the years had made me feel like a part of their family. Despite the late hour, I decided to take a nap, my exhausted body aching from the previous night's events. Although I had taken a long, hot shower, a faint odor from the sewers still clung to my hair.

In my sleep, I had a somewhat familiar dream. Claire and I were together in the flooded tunnel, but this time, there was no flashlight. Instead, a small pulsating light appeared at the end of the tunnel, accompanied by

Claire's voice calling out to me. Despite my efforts, each step felt like trudging through thick glue, making it impossible to reach the wooden door that faintly materialized.

Claire's voice grew fainter with each step, and the light blinded me when it intensified. I shielded my eyes, but the thick substance weighed me down, rendering me helpless. As drops of water fell, transforming into a downpour, the sound grew deafening, forcing me to close my eyes.

Abruptly, I woke up, drenched in sweat. The sound of running water caught my attention. It was strange because I had turned off the shower before falling asleep. Someone must have turned it on—perhaps Mrs. Volinsky or her husband checking the water pressure. However, their entry into my apartment seemed unlikely.

Gathering myself, I left my room to investigate. It was past six in the evening, with the sun already setting. Steam filled the bathroom as I approached, attempting to turn on the light switch, which didn't work. Opening the shower door, I discovered the lifeless body of Crosby lying face down, naked.

"Crosby?" I called out, but there was no response.

I had never given her a key to my apartment, so how had she gotten in? Why was she in my shower? It became apparent that someone had put her there.

"Crosby?" I tried again, but she remained unresponsive.

Have You Seen Me? My Name is Claire Hines

Turning off the shower, I gently touched her back. She felt icy cold. Realizing she was no longer alive, I pressed my fingers against her neck, confirming the grim truth.

Chapter 12

Empty Cage

"Gomez, it's Michael. You need to send a squad and an ambulance to my apartment. It's Crosby. I found her in my bathroom, and I think she's... Okay, I'll wait here."

After ending the call with Commissioner Gomez, I sat silently on the cold bathroom floor, my hands resting on the smooth white tiles. Confusion overwhelmed me as I tried to process how Crosby's body ended up in my apartment while I was asleep. Touching my arm, I confirmed that this was not a dream. I felt bewildered. How did she end up here?

Glancing at my cell phone, I saw that it was almost nine at night. Waking up to the sight of a dead FBI agent in my bathtub was not how I had hoped to start my day. Sorrow washed over me, and tears streamed down my face. I quickly packed a bag with clothes, anticipating that I might not be allowed back into my apartment as it was about to become a crime scene. Crosby's body was already showing signs of discoloration, indicating she had been dead for hours.

Seeing her lifeless form lying in my bathtub felt surreal. When I had arrived home and taken a shower earlier, she was not there. How did this happen? Moments later, the police, including Gomez, arrived at my apartment.

"Yup, that's her," Gomez declared, his voice tinged with remorse and sadness.

I remained silent, my mind racing with thoughts of the consequences. The presence of a dead FBI agent in my apartment would undoubtedly make me a prime suspect in Claire's disappearance. The media would have a field day with this.

"Okay, Michael, you better come with us. We need to get your statement before the media gets wind of this," Gomez instructed.

Being wide awake at this hour made me feel like a vampire. Normally, by eleven at night, I would be unwinding in bed after a long day of work. How I missed my normal routine. Ever since all of this began, my life had been far from ordinary. My job as a financial advisor had been put on hold since Claire went missing. I used to manage multiple financial accounts for various clients, including families and wealthy individuals like Michael

Fisher, who invested a substantial amount against my advice and lost a significant portion of his family's wealth. Despite having proof of my cautionary recommendations, his father blamed me for his son's financial downfall.

The incident garnered public attention, and it was a challenging pill to swallow. It was the first time something like this had happened to me, over three years ago. If the police asked about enemies, I would mention this family. No one else in my life was as angry with me as they were.

We entered the police station, where two officers escorted me into a cold room with a gray desk and three brown chairs. The walls were bare and white.

Have You Seen Me? My Name is Claire Hines

Gomez and the officer named Lorenzo entered the room.

Lorenzo greeted me and offered me a drink.

"Would you like some water or coffee?" he asked.

"Water would be good, thank you," I replied.

"I'll get it," Gomez said, leaving me alone with Officer Lorenzo.

We sat in silence, awaiting the commissioner's return. A few moments later, Gomez entered the room and handed me a plastic water bottle. Lorenzo opened his notepad and cleared his throat.

"Now, let's start from the beginning, shall we?" Lorenzo said.

I leaned forward in my chair, placing my arms on the table, feeling a mix of confidence and nervousness. This felt more like an interrogation than an interview.

"I'll tell you exactly what happened," I began.

Gomez focused his attention on me, and Lorenzo started taking notes.

"After I left here this morning, I went straight home. I had breakfast and took a shower. There were no bodies in the bathtub at that time, or I wouldn't have showered. Then I decided to take a nap, which ended up lasting several hours."

"What happened after you woke up?" Lorenzo asked, and Gomez continued scribbling in his notebook.

"I had a strange dream about Claire, and when I woke up, I heard the sound of the shower running. I distinctly remember turning it off before my nap."

Gomez stared at me skeptically, as if he found my story hard to believe. Hearing myself talk made me realize how unbelievable it sounded. I might as well have claimed that aliens placed Crosby's body in my bathtub.

"What did you do after you heard the shower running?" Gomez inquired.

I looked down at my water bottle, took a deep breath, and tried to convey honesty and conciseness, despite the absurdity of my story.

Have You Seen Me? My Name is Claire Hines

"After getting out of bed, I went to the bathroom and realized the lights weren't working. There was a lot of steam from the hot water. I turned off the hot water and saw Crosby lying naked in my bathtub, facing away from me."

"Hold on a minute," Gomez interrupted. "How did you see her if the lights weren't working?"

"I used the flashlight on my cell phone to find the faucet and shower knobs. That's when I noticed something in the bathtub. I shined the light and saw a naked woman lying there. It was at that moment I recognized her. After checking if she was alive, I called you."

Gomez clasped his hands together and brought them up to his face, lost in thought.

"Let me make sure I understand. You're telling us that someone entered your apartment while you were asleep, turned on the shower, and left Crosby's body in the bathtub. And you heard nothing?"

Have You Seen Me? My Name is Claire Hines

I shook my head. "No, I was genuinely exhausted from the previous night."

Gomez rubbed his eyes, while Lorenzo observed me silently.

"I understand how this looks, but I'm telling you the truth. I'm not involved in this," I insisted.

A knock on the door interrupted our conversation. "Come in," Gomez called out.

An officer entered and whispered something into Gomez's ear.

"Looks like you're off the hook, for now, Michael," Gomez said.

"I wouldn't lie to you, especially since I want to find Claire and whoever is responsible for all of this," I replied.

Have You Seen Me? My Name is Claire Hines

Chapter 13

The Package

The brown package sat on a table in the conference room. It appeared like any other package one would receive from an online order or a loved one. Wanted papers with photos of criminals and their bios adorned the wall, while a large map of the city, marked with pins and connecting lines, hung on a gray-colored wall.

"Don't touch the package. We need to bring in the bomb squad to ensure it's not dangerous!" Gomez ordered everyone out of the building as a precaution.

Before leaving the room, I noticed that the package was addressed to me. It had an unusual shape resembling an NFL football.

Outside, everyone stood waiting for the bomb squad to arrive. The breeze made it chilly, and I clutched a cup of coffee to keep warm.

"What do you think could be in there?" asked Officer Lancaster.

"Sergeant Lancaster," corrected Gomez. "Escort the bomb squad into the building and show them where the package is located."

"Yes, sir," replied the officer.

A group of heavily dressed officers followed Lancaster inside. Though Gomez didn't suspect it was a bomb, he wasn't taking any chances. The bomb squad members looked more like linebackers in their heavy tactical gear than police officers. Standing there, I felt anxious, not just because of the possibility of the package being a bomb, but also because it could contain Claire's remains.

The thought was morbid, but not knowing the intentions of the person behind it put me on edge. It didn't make sense. Why would they send a bomb to end my life in such a hurry? The kidnapper wanted to toy with me, reveling in their sense of power and control.

"Okay, we've confirmed there are no explosives inside. It's safe to open the package," said the bomb squad officer behind his protective mask. The squad members left the building, resembling futuristic astronauts.

We returned to the conference room, where the package sat peacefully on the table. I felt nervous about what I would find inside.

"Michael, would you like to open the box?" Gomez asked politely.

After putting on gloves to avoid leaving fingerprints, I nodded and approached the table with trepidation. I prepared myself and carefully opened the package. What I discovered inside changed everything. There were three items.

The first was a lock of hair, and I immediately recognized it as Claire's—her passionate red hair shining beneath the artificial lights. This gave me hope, as it meant whoever sent it was with her, implying she might still be alive.

"A lock of hair?" Gomez asked, his hand resting beneath his mouth.

"Yes, I believe it belongs to Claire. Take it and run tests to confirm, although I'm certain it's hers," I said, handing the lock of hair to him.

Gomez agreed and passed it to a nearby officer. "Take this to the lab and compare it to the DNA samples recovered from her blood."

The officer took the hair and swiftly left the room. The next item in the package was a photo of a lighthouse standing alone on a long, thin pier. It felt like a metaphor for my life since Claire's disappearance.

"Does anyone recognize this place?" I asked, holding up the photo of the lighthouse.

"Pass it around, maybe someone will know," suggested Gomez.

As the photo circulated, discussions filled the room, but no certainties were reached. The image of the lighthouse, standing in solitude before a vast body of water, made me wonder if it was located at Lake Michigan.

Have You Seen Me? My Name is Claire Hines

Considering that all the incidents so far had occurred in Chicago, it seemed likely.

"I think this is somewhere nearby, probably in the city," I declared.

This moment felt oddly reminiscent of opening presents at a birthday party. The officers behind me were like friends witnessing me unwrap my gifts. However, this was no celebration. The final item I found was a small white origami paper shaped like a fish, presumably another message from the person behind all this.

Gomez instructed forensics to run tests for prints on the note and the photograph.

"We need to find this lighthouse before it's too late," he said.

"We'll find her, Michael, don't worry. We need to figure out where this lighthouse is. There are several like it throughout Chicago," assured Gomez.

"I know where it is," one of the officers proclaimed after examining the photo. "It's near that new area on Randolph

Have You Seen Me? My Name is Claire Hines

Street and Columbus Drive. The city has been renovating that area with million-dollar condos and lofts."

Gomez looked at the officer, intrigued. "And how do you know this, Detective Winters?"

Winters, who could pass as my younger sister, appeared no older than nineteen. Her brown hair was tied in a knot under her baseball cap.

"My boyfriend tried to convince me to buy a place there. I remember seeing a lighthouse across from Lake Shore Drive. But..." she hesitated.

"But what?" I asked.

"Well, the note mentioned a light that dimly shines."

"She's right, Michael," Gomez added. "It could be a trap, especially since the killer wants you to come alone."

Ignoring Gomez, I said, "But that could be Claire. The light might have been turned off intentionally. And if she's at the top of the lighthouse, the light would blind her or create a silhouette."

Silence fell upon the room.

Have You Seen Me? My Name is Claire Hines

"Regardless, I have to go alone, and I have to go now. Whoever sent us this package wanted me to see it today, which means they want me to come tonight."

"Why don't we wait for the test results to come back? We need to be certain it's Claire," suggested Gomez.

As stubborn as I was, Gomez was right. We needed to be sure this wasn't a trap.

"Whoever is up there, Claire or not," I said, "They need our help, and they need it now."

Chapter 14

Answers

Several hours later, the sun had begun to set. We spent the rest of the morning and afternoon waiting for the fingerprint test results from the note. The hair analysis would take longer, but the FBI Forensics team expedited the process for the fingerprints. Playing the waiting game was difficult, and my impatience consumed me like a disease.

Officer Winters, who sat beside me at the conference table, observed my knee bouncing and fidgeting unintentionally. I was too absorbed in planning to notice how I might be annoying her with my restlessness.

Leaving under the cover of night made more sense. I had to go alone, as any presence of others might endanger Claire.

"We're going to wire you up with a camera. Both will be disguised as buttons on your shirt, so keep your jacket

Have You Seen Me? My Name is Claire Hines

open. Whoever you meet won't suspect a thing," assured Winters.

Running on a mixture of caffeine and sleepless nights, I engaged in conversation with the officer to distract myself.

"How long have you and your boyfriend been together?" I asked.

She leaned back in her chair, studying my outfit and the hidden recording devices.

"About a year now, on and off," she replied.

"On and off?" I inquired.

Satisfied with my appearance, Winters didn't immediately answer. "You look good. I don't think anyone will notice your wire. Yeah, we had a rocky relationship."

"What was rocky about it?" I asked.

"He was full of doubts about us and what he wanted," she responded.

"I understand. It's tough to find the right person," I smiled at her.

Have You Seen Me? My Name is Claire Hines

"I'm not sure if you can tell, Michael, but I'm not the best girlfriend, being a cop. Most of my time is spent here helping others, like yourself."

Her honesty struck me. I hadn't considered how much time people in her profession dedicate to their work, solving crimes and handling cases.

"I... um... thank..." I started to say.

"No need to thank me," she interrupted. "I'm just doing my job. Plus, we need to get this bastard for what he did to the team. He's not going to get away from me!"

I admired Winters. Her personality reminded me of a tough cop who took no nonsense from anyone. She also seemed capable of holding her own in physical conflicts.

"Good news... Oh wow, look at you! You look ready," declared Gomez as he entered the office, holding a thin green folder which I assumed contained the fingerprint results.

Have You Seen Me? My Name is Claire Hines

"He does!" Winters chimed in, making a few last adjustments to the bulletproof vest hidden beneath my clothing.

"Michael, you look ready, and you should be. The results aren't ready yet."

"I have Officer Winters to thank for that."

"Please, call me Rebecca, Winters interjected.

I looked at Gomez, wanting to ask when the results would be ready. He wore a white shirt and red tie that complemented his black slacks. The Commissioner knew how to dress and carry himself well—maybe that's why the department looked up to him. He was born to lead, and he did it with pride.

"Do we have any idea who's behind this?" I asked, adjusting the leather jacket on my shoulders.

"Too tight?" Winters asked, inspecting the jacket.

"Ah, so now he's calling you Rebecca? Nobody gets to call you by your first name, not even me, and I'm your boss!" Gomez chuckled lightly.

Have You Seen Me? My Name is Claire Hines

It was the first time I saw him with a playful demeanor. Gomez had been serious thus far, but seeing him banter with the officer eased my nervousness. It was refreshing to witness lightheartedness, even during such a challenging case.

"I like this one, Commish. He's a nice guy," declared Winters.

Gomez smiled, then looked at me. "You're in good hands, Michael. Winters is going with you, and she'll look after you."

"What about the prints? Do you know when they'll be ready?" I asked.

Gomez's smile faded. "Unfortunately, no, I don't know," his voice turned dry and serious again.

"But don't worry, we'll catch this person. If the note they sent you is accurate, this will end tonight. All the answers to our questions lie in that lighthouse."

The certainty in Gomez's voice boosted my confidence. Tonight would determine Claire's fate, and I held faith that she was still alive.

"Listen, tonight you're going in alone, but we'll be nearby. The team will monitor your every move. We'll be on standby. I don't want any mistakes. We're doing this by the book."

Winters nodded in agreement. "Michael, if something goes wrong, all you need to say is 'Friday night lights.'"

"Friday night lights," I repeated.

"That's correct. After you say those words, Winters will storm in and rescue you. The rest of the team will be nearby."

"I'll be your shadow tonight. Don't worry, Michael," Winters said, resting both her hands on my shoulders. "I'll be a ninja." She knelt before me as I sat in the chair. The gear felt snug and tight, hugging my body. Her hazel eyes met mine directly. "I'll protect you tonight, okay? I'm sorry you're in this situation, but we need you to be strong."

Have You Seen Me? My Name is Claire Hines

I weakly smiled.

"I understand," I said. "Thank you both for having my back tonight. I couldn't have made it this far."

"Just in case things take a turn for the worse, take this," said Gomez, offering a small revolver. "We know you have military training."

"I better not," I declined. If I go in armed, it might jeopardize the entire mission."

Both Gomez and Winters exchanged glances.

"Fair enough," Winters added. "We just want you to be safe and careful out there. This could be a trap."

Have You Seen Me? My Name is Claire Hines

Chapter 15

The Lighthouse

A sliver of the crescent moon watched from behind the clouds on this freezing night. A steady breeze rolled by as we approached the pier, with the unlit lighthouse looming in the distance like a ghostly shadow. Waves crashed against the pier, leaving droplets of water on my tactical jacket and face. I covered my face with a black tactical gaiter, the soft material providing some warmth.

As we walked together down the pier, Winters asked if I was nervous. I looked at her and shook my head, my face also concealed behind a mask. "I'm feeling a little anxious," I replied.

"Don't worry, I'll be here waiting for you. If anything happens in there, just say the words," she reassured me.

When we reached halfway to the lighthouse, it was time to part ways. Winters hid behind a group of large jagged rocks and explained the plan.

Have You Seen Me? My Name is Claire Hines

"I'll wait here. Remember, if you need me, just say the words. I'll go in twenty minutes from now, so try to stall them."

I watched as she took out a small device from her vest pocket—a small earpiece. She handed it to me, resembling a tiny insect. "Place this in your ear and speak freely," she instructed. "No one will see it, but it's strong enough for you to be heard."

I inserted the small device into my right ear canal, feeling its hard rubber-like texture. "Okay, now say something," she said.

"Something," I responded, and she chuckled. "Cute, okay, that should do it," she said.

I nodded and turned away, but she stopped me. "Before you go..." she began. Without further words, she gave me a tight hug.

"Whatever happens in there, know that I'll be with you. After you enter the lighthouse, I'll wait fifteen minutes before coming in."

"I thought you said twenty?" I questioned.

She shook her head. "I changed my mind. You have fifteen, so make every second count!"

Feeling slightly awkward from the unexpected hug, I thanked her and she urged me to get going. I hid my face beneath my gaiter and sprinted away, finding comfort in that brief moment between us amidst the uncertainties ahead.

The closer I got, the more the lighthouse appeared like a black phantom, with a sense of malevolence emanating from its top. It felt as though something or someone was watching and waiting for me. Across the lake, the infamous Chicago skyline stood, partly covered by fog and clouds, while the lights of the office buildings glowed in the windows of smaller structures. I couldn't help but imagine people living their daily lives, driven by love— the same force that had brought me here. I needed to know if my love was still alive.

"Michael?" Winters' soft voice reached my right ear.

Have You Seen Me? My Name is Claire Hines

"Yeah?" I whispered.

"Just checking to make sure you're okay," she said.

"I'm fine. It's just taking me longer than expected to reach the lighthouse. I'm feeling..." I paused, searching for the right word.

"Scared?" she suggested.

"Yeah," I replied. "Scared."

"Don't worry, I'm with you. I made a promise to bring you back in one piece. I'll keep that promise to Gomez, myself, and especially you."

"Rebecca?"

"Yes, Michael?"

"Why are you helping me? I don't want you to say it's just because of your job. There's more to this, isn't there?"

"Crosby was my friend when I first started out on the force. She was there for me and the only person I could confide in. Now she's gone, forever. Whoever killed her will pay for that."

Have You Seen Me? My Name is Claire Hines

A cold shiver ran down my back as the wind picked up, sprinkling more lake water on me. The shadowy figure of the lighthouse grew more visible as I approached.

"I'm at the entrance," I declared.

"Roger that. Check around the doorway for any booby traps," advised Winters.

"Okay."

I turned on my small tactical flashlight and inspected the entrance. Its white-blue light revealed two large, faded red doors. One of the doors was slightly ajar, indicating they were expecting me.

"I don't see any wires or traps. One of the doors is slightly open. I'm going in," I relayed.

"Roger," Winters responded softly, her voice carrying a hint of frustration. She wasn't fond of being a bystander while I played the role of a guinea pig.

I carefully pushed the door forward, causing it to creak against the metal floor. Whoever awaited me inside now knew I was there. A cold draft filled the air as I entered the lighthouse, aiming my flashlight upward. A spiral grated staircase sat at the center, its twisted design casting eerie shadows against the metal walls. There was nothing else to see, so it was time to begin my ascent. The stairwell reminded me of a twisty slide I used to ride at a public park, though this nightmare was far from enjoyable.

The railing creaked and felt unstable, and with every step, a lurid, rigid metallic sound echoed through the hollow walls. I couldn't say I felt comfortable in my current situation.

"Winters," I whispered. "I'm going up the staircase."

"Roger that. Be careful, Michael."

Have You Seen Me? My Name is Claire Hines

Chapter 16

The Lantern Room

After climbing the dizzying staircase, I reached the top of the lighthouse, exhausted but determined. My heart pounded in my chest, and sweat soaked my bulletproof vest beneath my shirt. It was an unexpected workout.

Outside the lantern room, I found a closed wooden door. Surprisingly, there were no booby traps. It seemed that whoever was waiting for me inside wanted me to arrive safely. I turned off my flashlight and pushed open the heavy door, the sound of wood against steel echoing through the lighthouse. They knew I had arrived.

Entering the circular room, track lights suddenly illuminated from above. Unpainted metal walls surrounded me, and a damp, moldy smell lingered in the air. Red letters painted on the walls caught my attention, though they were difficult to make out. Among them, the word "HAHA" appeared multiple times in red, resembling blood.

As I looked around, the sound of a squeaking rat distracted me. On the opposite side of the room stood the man I had encountered the night Claire was taken. He resembled a ghost, silently watching me. Seeing him ignited a bloodthirsty rage within me, but I fought to maintain my composure.

The man wore a ragged trench coat and had a filthy, wrinkled face covered in white facial hair. His smile revealed a horrific mouth with few remaining yellow-stained teeth, resembling jagged stalagmites. In one of his gray, fingerless gloved hands, he held a menacing carving knife, rusted and seemingly bloodstained.

Beside him, a naked woman hung lifelessly, suspended by chains connected to metal cuffs on her limbs. He tapped her body, emitting a dry, raspy laugh from his frail frame. His brown pants covered his thin legs, but they were full of holes.

Opening his mouth wider, he revealed a severed tongue, explaining the dreadful sound of his laughter. Tempted to say the code word, I resisted and silently

Have You Seen Me? My Name is Claire Hines

stared. It became clear that the suspended woman was Claire, savagely hung like a macabre decoration. I wondered if she was still alive.

Carefully, I approached him, causing his laughter to cease. The lights abruptly turned off, plunging me into darkness. I reached for my flashlight, but the man tackled me to the metal floor before I could use it. The sudden attack left me speechless and disoriented.

His hot breath and spittle rained down on my face as I managed to ask, "Who are you?"

"Mammon," he replied.

Confused, I questioned him further, but only received more laughter in response. I pushed him away, and he jumped back, landing with certainty on the metal floor. His grotesque laughter filled the circular room like that of a ravenous jackal, his voice cracking and squealing.

"What have you done to her?" I cried out.

I ignited my flashlight and aimed it at him, watching as he hastily climbed up the white metal ladder.

Have You Seen Me? My Name is Claire Hines

Determined not to let him escape, I declared, "You're not getting away from me!" and followed him up the ladder.

The lantern room was a small, circular space with a massive light fixture encased in glass at its center. With his back to an open window, Mammon repeated the word "Piamon."

"What are you doing?" I demanded.

"Mammon," he repeated once more, wicked laughter escaping his lips.

He charged at me again, and this time I did my best to resist his attack. However, he pushed me back, causing my head to slam into the glass. Thankfully, the glass remained intact, but my consciousness began to fade. As my vision blurred, I whispered the words, "Friday... night... lights..."

Have You Seen Me? My Name is Claire Hines

Chapter 17

The Investigation Begins

Multiple helicopters flew overhead, their spotlights piercing the darkness and illuminating the lantern room at the top of the lighthouse. The weak glow of the bulb was overshadowed by the blinding light. Slowly, I opened my eyes, momentarily disoriented.

"There you are," Winters said, crouching beside me and offering her assistance.

A throbbing pain radiated through my brain and skull, and my balance was unsteady from the attack. Gradually, I began to remember where I was.

"Mammon," I uttered simply, but Winters ignored my comment and helped me down the thin metal ladder.

Outside the lighthouse, a group of reporters anxiously awaited Gomez's statement. They resembled a pack of ravenous wolves, chattering and restless. Despite the increasing wind and crashing waves, they huddled together on the nearby pier, separated by yellow police tape bearing the words "DO NOT ENTER."

Inside the dome-shaped room, letters were painted on the walls. Winters meticulously copied them into her notepad, even though they appeared scrambled and lacked vowels. My instincts told me that it was another riddle.

Below, forensic officers ascended the spiral staircase to collect evidence and investigate the crime scene. One of the officers declared that it would take several days to determine what had transpired.

Meanwhile, other officers carefully brought down the suspended woman, treating her like a sadistic display. I sat on the grated metal floor, observing as they delicately handled the lifeless body with gloved hands.

"Easy now," cautioned one of the officers as they laid her down and a paramedic checked her vitals.

"Strange," the paramedic remarked.

"What is?" Winters inquired.

Have You Seen Me? My Name is Claire Hines

"This woman... She..." the paramedic hesitated.

"What?" I asked from across the room.

"She's not real," the paramedic replied. "There's no pulse. Nothing. The epidermis is made from…silicon."

She picked up the upper half of the body, removing the wig to reveal a hairless doll. Gasps of shock and disbelief escaped the officers nearby, and Gomez entered the room, noticing the peculiar sight.

"What the hell is that?" he exclaimed.

"That's what I found when I entered the room, along with the man," I explained.

"Man?" Gomez questioned. "Winters, did you see anyone else when you arrived?"

Winters shook her head. "No, sir. I found Michael unconscious in the lantern room. I did see an open window, but jumping from this height into the lake would be fatal."

Gomez frowned. "That's why you have doubts. I believe anyone can survive the impossible. I've seen addicts survive impossible jumps due to their drug-induced

Have You Seen Me? My Name is Claire Hines

delusions. Their brains turn them into superheroes. Alright, we need a team to search the lake and the shore. If there's a body, we'll find it. Michael, can you provide a description of the man you encountered?"

I described the man I presumed to be Mammon to the team.

"Mammon, huh?" Gomez mused. "I'll contact headquarters to see if we have any records on him. Get some prints off that doll. What the hell is going on here?" He pointed at the wall. "Is someone writing an alphabet here? What does it mean?"

"That's what we're trying to figure out, sir," Winters responded. "It appears to be another riddle."

"Great, another riddle. Who the hell is Mammon?" Gomez rubbed his tired eyes.

"He's the one who attacked me," I answered.

"Don't worry, Michael. We'll find out who this guy is and apprehend him! I need to make a statement."

Have You Seen Me? My Name is Claire Hines

Gomez left the room to address the news reporters outside the lighthouse. Winters helped me up and offered me a place to stay.

"Do you have somewhere to go?" she asked.

I shook my head. "No, I don't."

"Well, you can stay at my place. I have a couch with your name on it."

"That's kind of you, but I don't want to impose."

"It's no problem. It'll take them a few days to sort out this mess anyway. We can swing by your place on the way and grab some of your things."

"Okay, as long as it's not a hassle."

"It's not. Come on."

I followed Winters down the spiral staircase and emerged from the lighthouse. Gomez had just finished his update for the reporters, who eagerly bombarded me with questions as I made my way through the crowd.

"Michael!" a reporter yelled. "Do you have anything to say about Claire?"

Cameras pointed at me like mechanical eyes capturing my every move, but I ignored them and continued walking amidst the sea of police and reporters.

"Are you really behind all of this?" another reporter shouted.

Though I wanted to respond, Winters ushered me into an unmarked squad car nearby.

"Just ignore them," she advised. "They'll ask anything for a story. Those reporters are nothing but a hungry pack of wolves. They'll do anything for a scoop."

Her words provided some reassurance, but I couldn't help feeling irked by the reporter's audacious question. Was I really the one behind Claire's disappearance? What could I possibly gain from it? I wanted to protest, to address the question, but Winters was right. Dwelling on it would serve no purpose.

Have You Seen Me? My Name is Claire Hines

Chapter 18

Sister

We left the scene and drove toward my apartment when my phone vibrated. Winters sat in the front while another detective steered the unmarked squad car.

"We should be arriving at your apartment soon, Michael. I have two officers there now waiting for us," Winters said as I felt my phone go off again.

"Okay," I answered and looked at my phone. "Amanda is calling."

"Amanda?"

"She is Claire's sister. Maybe she saw me leaving the lighthouse on the evening news since it was live." I answered the phone, "Hello?"

A heavy breath filled the other end.

"Is anyone there?"

The call abruptly ended.

"Something wrong?" Winters asked. She turned and leaned against the leather seat to look at me.

Have You Seen Me? My Name is Claire Hines

"That was weird. The call just ended," I answered.

"Amanda did not say anything?"

"No. I heard breathing but…"

My phone vibrated again, but this time it was a text message from Amanda.

"I saw you on the news. I am not ready to repent. You have the clues. I am at your apartment. Come to your room. Best do it soon."

"Michael? What is it?" Winters asked while I stared at my phone, continuously reading the message.

"A cryptic text message," I replied.

"What do you mean?" Winters asked.

"The message is weird," I repeated.

"What does it say?"

I repeated the message aloud.

"The two officers at your apartment! They could be walking into a trap! Come in Reed, Vance?"

Static from the walkie-talkie filled the car.

"They are not answering, we need to get there fast!" Winters declared.

Have You Seen Me? My Name is Claire Hines

Ironically, we were already on our way to my apartment to pick up my essential belongings. This Mammon made me dread my apartment now. It was my sanctuary, my happy place that helped me escape from the stresses of life.

But now, the apartment is the center of my stress. The irony. They have ruined my only sanctuary.

We arrived at my apartment, and I hastily exited the car from the backseat and noticed the lights were off.

"I'll go check it out. Stay here, Vasquez," Winters said as she exited the passenger side of the car.

The driver, whose last name was Vasquez, protested at her fellow officer's command, "No, I'll go, stay here with Michael in case Mammon comes out of the apartment building."

Winters looked at the officer. "But, Vasquez, I…"

"Don't argue with me," Vasquez said. She slammed the car door. "I'm going in. Call for backup now."

Winters nodded and looked at me with worry. I stayed quiet as she entered the building. A light breeze surrounded us as I stood there quietly, staring at the dark windows of my apartment. Winters radioed for backup, then waited for the officer's update.

"Winters, come in," Vasquez said through the radio.

"Yeah, I read you, what's the status?" Winters responded.

"There are two bodies here. It's Reed and Vance. Weird, the lights aren't working either. There's a trail of blood leading into Michael's room. I am going to investigate, over and out."

Winters paced around like an anxious panther. She wanted to back up her partner.

"Get me Gomez. Where is my backup? I need it now!" Winters yelled at the dispatcher. She nearly slammed the walkie-talkie into the asphalt.

I wanted to say something to comfort her, but my attention remained fixated on my room. From this vantage point, my room appeared dark and demented, almost as if it were haunted or swimming in melancholy. Who knew how long it would be until backup arrived? I wanted to go in there since this was my apartment.

"I found a body. It's a woman. The description matches Claire except for her eyes and hair. The eyes are green and the hair is curly, and it looks like she's been dead for a few hours," Vasquez responded.

"Curly hair and resembles Claire? That would be her sister, Amanda. Claire has straight hair," I said to Winters, who relayed my message. I could feel my eyes swelling with sadness.

"I'm going to try to move the body out of here. I don't think Michael should come up here."

"Winters, tell her I have a bag under the bed in my room," I said.

"Hold on, Vasquez. Michael needs to say something to you." She handed me her walkie-talkie. "Here, talk to her."

"I have a go bag under the bed in my room. It is filled with clothes and other essential items," I said.

"Got it. I am going to open one of the windows and toss this sucker out. Catch it, okay?"

Have You Seen Me? My Name is Claire Hines

"I will," I answered. I returned Winters her walkie-talkie and sprinted toward the five-story building.

"Be careful," Winters advised.

Vasquez quickly grabbed my bag, then opened my bedroom window and tossed it. I caught it just in time, despite the bag feeling a bit heavier than I remembered. Afterward, I returned to the car and tossed my bag onto the backseat.

"Wait," I said aloud as I realized something from the cryptic text message.

"Okay, I am going to try to remove the body now," Vasquez stated through the radio.

"Winters, the message said if I come into my room, I will meet certain doom."

Winters was flummoxed by my statement. "Yeah, so what? We found the certain doom. It was Amanda and the two officers."

"No," I replied. "What if there was more to this certain doom? What if there's another trap inside my apartment?"

Have You Seen Me? My Name is Claire Hines

"Oh my gosh! Maybe she shouldn't touch anything. Who knows what's inside your bag!"

I looked at Winters and felt nervous standing beside the car.

"Vasquez! Whatever you do, please don't move the body!" Winters pleaded.

But it was too late.

"I already pulled her body out of the closet. There was a rope around her neck that someone tied. Wait, what's this? There's another rope around her wrist, and it's attached to. Oh no! Oh my g—"

Vasquez was abruptly cut off as the windows of my apartment shattered, followed by a deafening explosion. Shards of glass rained down along with a large plume of flames and smoke. The force of the explosion knocked me against the car, followed by Winters, who landed in my arms. I lay on the cold and damp pavement while still holding onto the officer. My vision became blurry as my head ached terribly from the impact.

Have You Seen Me? My Name is Claire Hines

A fiery fury continued violently spewing out of my bedroom window like an urban volcano. The sounds of emergency vehicle sirens grew in the distance. My vision became foggy as the sirens grew.

Everything I had in that apartment, including my furniture, clothing, picture frames, and memories, were all instantly taken away. What I owned was in that apartment, and now it burned like my last bits of hopefulness. I yearned for all of this to end. It was at that moment when I reluctantly accepted that Claire must have met the same fate as her sister did that night.

Chapter 19

Unexpected Visitor

When I was a child, I believed my parents would live forever, and the concept of death felt foreign to me. The thought of losing loved ones, such as my parents, had never crossed my mind. However, when someone we truly love dies, it leaves an emotional scar.

I was abruptly brought back to consciousness by an intense pain in my head. The explosion in my apartment had knocked out the streetlights, and I saw a man standing over us with his back turned. He silently gazed at the damage caused by the flames that engulfed the majority of the building, including my bedroom.

The man eventually noticed I was no longer unconscious and approached us slowly. Winters remained unconscious, still on top of me. I attempted to move, but the weight of her body and the persistent ache in my head made it challenging. He stood over me, gazing down with a smile stretching across his face, resembling the sliver of moonlight above us.

Reaching into the pocket of his trench coat, the man extracted a small envelope. His hands were covered in black latex gloves, reminiscent of what a mortician would wear. He glanced at the envelope and flicked it at me indifferently, as if it were a business card from someone he didn't care about. The envelope landed on Winters, who remained unconscious. Arrogantly, the man turned away and walked in the opposite direction of the approaching sirens. This was the person responsible for everything: Claire's disappearance, the murders, and the fire that ravaged throughout the night.

The red and blue lights of the emergency vehicles flickered and grew brighter as they arrived. Winters groaned and slowly shifted her body, causing the envelope to fall onto the pavement beside us.

"Winters, he was here. I saw him," I whispered.

"Saw... Who? What are you talking about?" Winters slowly regained consciousness.

Have You Seen Me? My Name is Claire Hines

"I saw him! He gave me this," I replied, reaching out to grab the envelope.

"What is that?"

"He gave it to me!" I answered. Paramedics and other emergency crew swiftly exited their vehicles and approached us.

"Are you hurt? Can you move, sir?" one of the paramedics asked me.

"No, I can move, but please help her. Her name is Officer Winters."

"Officer Winters? My name is Theo. Let me help you up," he said, attempting to assist Winters.

"I'm fine," Winters stated, pushing Theo away as she regained her composure.

I felt dried blood on the back of my head from the impact with the squad car's window. Moments later, Gomez arrived on the scene.

"Holy hell. What happened here? Are you two all right?"

Winters shrugged off the soreness in her body. "I'm fine, still feeling a bit lightheaded, but I landed on Michael, my savior," she answered, affectionately smiling at me.

"Yeah, I seem to have taken the brunt of the damage for both of us," I added, eliciting a chuckle from her that momentarily eased my headache.

I decided to inform Gomez about what had transpired.

"Sir, I saw him. I saw the man behind all of this."

An expression of perplexity crossed Gomez's weathered face.

"Where did you see him?" Gomez approached me as I sat on the curb near the damaged squad car, smoke billowing from my apartment into the early dawn-lit sky.

"He stood not too far from where you are."

As I spoke, Gomez examined the pavement near his feet.

"He left me this, but I haven't opened it yet. I wanted to wait until we were back at the station."

Gomez knelt in front of me to be at eye-level.

"Do you remember what he looked like?" Gomez inquired.

Have You Seen Me? My Name is Claire Hines

"Kind of. I was still feeling the effects of the explosion. But he wore black gloves. He knew not to leave fingerprints."

"Black gloves?"

"Yeah," I replied.

"Look, Michael, I know you want to open it now. So, let's see what this person wrote!" Winters interjected.

I nodded and tore open the top of the envelope, reminiscent of a child opening a birthday card. Inside was another riddle:

I stood with you watching the flames,

Together both our lives changed.

Mine for the worst and yours for the better,

Take your time while reading this letter.

You will find the next clue,

I will be waiting for you.

At the bottom of the riddle, there were a set of stained letters, presumably in red ink. They resembled the ones found in the lighthouse but were vowels. I retrieved

Have You Seen Me? My Name is Claire Hines

my notebook and realized this was the second half of the
puzzle from the lighthouse.

"Look! This note has a set of letters, but these are vowels!"
Gomez and Winters examined the letter.

"We should go back to the station and figure this out!" I
exclaimed excitedly.

"No, go with Winters to her place and get some rest,
Michael," Gomez dismissed.

Although I wanted to protest, the need for sleep
overwhelmed me. My body and head throbbed with pain,
so I acquiesced to his advice.

"Winters," I said, "If it's okay with you, I w—" Before I could
finish my sentence, she helped me up.

"Let's go, Michael."

"Don't worry," Gomez assured us. "We will clean up this
mess and regroup at the station in the morning. Come by,
and I should have the results from the hair and blood
samples we found at the lighthouse."

Have You Seen Me? My Name is Claire Hines

Chapter 20

Dreams

I felt my heart break as I watched my personal belongings burn away, lost like forgotten memories. At least I had a temporary place to stay. Apart from the photos on my phone, everything inside my duffle bag was all I had left.

"I'm sorry about what happened to you tonight, Michael," Winters said to me as we entered her studio apartment.

"Thank you again for letting me crash here tonight," I replied, removing my jacket and placing it near a vintage-looking tan loveseat in the living room.

"This is going to be your bed for tonight," she gestured towards the loveseat. It looked like it belonged in a trash dumpster, but in situations like these, beggars can't be choosers.

"Great," I replied, hoping not to sound ungrateful or sarcastic.

She smiled. "Trust me, that couch is a lot more comfortable than it looks. I've had this thing since my college days. Sit down, I'll start dinner. I hope you're in the mood for spaghetti."

I smiled back at Winters and sat down on the couch. "Spaghetti sounds great."

We sat at the small kitchen table and ate in silence. The events of the night had taken a toll on both of us. The little conversation we did have mostly revolved around our families. I told her about my parents' passing a few years ago, how I met Claire, the proposal, and my job.

She shared stories about her previous boyfriend, her parents, and her life in America. Born in Cuba, her father was Cuban, while her mother was Syrian.

As much as we both wanted to continue talking, it was getting late. Moreover, the stress from earlier had left us feeling weary.

After the meal, I laid down on the soft couch and fell asleep without hesitation. As my mind drifted into another world, I found myself on a ship out at sea. The waves rocked the vessel violently, as if a god were playing

with a toy. I gripped the railing of the stern, peering out at

the sea. Beside me, the man from the lighthouse

appeared, screaming out a plate full of gibberish. Claire

was there too; at least, I could hear her calling me. She

was in pain and filled with jealousy, her anger lashing out. I

could hear her voice filled with fury, accusing me and

Winters. *"Michael, how could you?"*

Chapter 21

Nightmares

I woke up drenched in sweat, still haunted by her angry voice echoing in my head. The room was dark, lit only by occasional flashes of lightning. The window shades did a poor job of blocking the streetlights, revealing random objects with each lightning flash. My back ached, as if I had slept on a hardwood floor.

A light turned on in the apartment building across, catching my attention. Peering through the shades, I saw a man with white hair staring in my direction. Another lightning flash signaled the approaching storm, sending a chill down my spine. Who was this guy?

Struggling to see him clearly, I assumed he was just a nosy neighbor. Sitting on the couch, I checked my phone and saw it was four in the morning—an odd time to be awake. Another flash momentarily illuminated the room, casting the silhouette of the neighbor on the walls.

Have You Seen Me? My Name is Claire Hines

Curiosity compelled me to return to the window. To my surprise, he was still there, watching me. I decided to greet him, thinking he might be awake due to a restless night. To my unease, he waved back, mimicking my movements like a reflection.

Feeling creeped out, I was interrupted by Winters entering the living room, turning on a vintage-looking lamp with a stained-glass shade. She asked about my waving, and I explained about the man across the building. Intrigued, she joined me at the window but saw no one there.

As I gazed out, the room suddenly appeared vacant, adding to the strangeness. Winters suggested I get some sleep, assuring me she was there to make sure I was okay. I thanked her, and as she left, I returned to the uncomfortable loveseat and fell asleep without hesitation.

Moments later, I awoke, struggling to keep my heavy eyelids open. I heard the slow movement of the doorknob, as if someone was trying to open the front door.

Have You Seen Me? My Name is Claire Hines

I attempted to call out to Winters but found myself voiceless. The door opened, revealing the man from the lighthouse, covered in char and soot, with glowing red eyes. Frozen in fear, he gripped my neck with his burnt hands, searing my flesh and suffocating me.

*** Rebecca ***

Knowing he was in the other room made me feel safer. It hadn't been an easy month with the breakup, losing my partner, and developing feelings for a guy whose fiancée was missing. Telling him would only complicate things further, so I kept it to myself.

It was already six in the morning, my usual time to wake up. Restless from the events of the previous night, I felt the need to wake Michael, who was sleeping on the loveseat. Something seemed off about him, so I gently shook his body. He woke up startled, as if he had seen a ghost.

Have You Seen Me? My Name is Claire Hines

Concerned, I asked if he was alright, and he explained he had been having a nightmare. He thanked me, saying that I had saved his life in the dream, which had felt all too real.

Chapter 22

The Puzzle – Part 1

After Winters cooked a hearty breakfast of white rice, black beans, fish, and plantains, we headed to the police station to meet with Commissioner Gomez. My goal was to decipher the letters left behind in the lighthouse and the night my apartment was destroyed.

We arrived at the station just after nine in the morning, and some officers and detectives were already occupied with my case. Gomez stood in the meeting room, facing a wall covered with photos from the crime scenes, including myself, Claire, and the puzzle found at the lighthouse. A paper with a list of victims' names, including Claire's at the top, broke my heart.

"Sorry we're late," I apologized.

"It's okay, Winters. I'm glad both you and Michael are here. I was briefing the team on last night's events. Unfortunately, everything was destroyed, and we lost some good officers," Gomez informed us.

Have You Seen Me? My Name is Claire Hines

"I understand, sir," I replied.

"Michael, I hope you're well-rested because today we're going to work on locating Mammon. I also want to know more about the man you saw outside your apartment. Was it the same person from the lighthouse?" Gomez inquired.

"I'm not certain, sir. I didn't get a clear look at his face, but he seemed younger than the man from the lighthouse. And there was something else," I explained.

"What would that be?" Gomez asked.

"He could speak. The man from the lighthouse couldn't," I answered.

We took our seats, trying to push aside the haunting dream from the previous night. The image of the charred man with demonic red eyes was etched in my memory, making it hard to forget. I took a deep breath, focusing my thoughts on happier times with Claire at the beach, while Gomez continued to discuss the events from last night.

"Seymore Bronson, that was his name. He attacked Michael at the lighthouse," Gomez announced.

Have You Seen Me? My Name is Claire Hines

The name caught my attention, sounding vaguely familiar,

but I couldn't recall where I had heard it before.

"Does that name ring a bell?" Gomez asked me.

"It does, but I'm not entirely sure why," I replied.

Gomez rubbed his chin, deep in thought. "Hmm, alright. I

believe we should investigate your clients. Perhaps it's

someone you dealt with at work. Did you have any

financial dealings with someone named Seymore?"

"I'm sorry, sir, but I don't remember," I answered.

"Focus on the puzzle, Michael. I'll look into your clients and

see if I find any connections," Gomez advised.

"Okay, I'll write down all the letters and try to make sense

of them," I said.

"Alright, I'll get us some tea," Winters offered.

I watched her leave the room before grabbing my

notepad. Gomez followed her, and I took the opportunity to

jot down the letters. They continued their conversation in

the kitchen while the other officers conversed amongst

Have You Seen Me? My Name is Claire Hines

themselves. The tension between Gomez and Winters seemed palpable.

"Winters, can I talk to you for a moment?" Gomez asked.

"Sure, what's on your mind?" she replied, placing two mugs in the microwave.

"Does Michael seem... neurotic to you?" Gomez inquired.

"Neurotic? I don't know if I'd use that word, but he does seem stressed. I can understand considering everything he's been through. Wait, what are you suggesting? You don't think he's responsible for all of this, do you?" Winters responded with a sharp tone.

Gomez leaned on the granite counter, observing Winters as she removed the tea bags. "I don't know. It just doesn't add up. It's highly unlikely for him to kidnap his own fiancée."

"Exactly," Winters retorted.

The tension between them escalated. "Look, all I'm saying is to keep an eye on him, okay? Don't get too close. I see the way you look at him, Rebecca," Gomez cautioned.

Winters scowled at the use of her first name. "Fine.

Whatever you say, sir," she replied curtly and stormed out

of the kitchen, returning to the conference room.

"Here's some green tea with honey," Winters said, handing

me the cup. The warmth seeped into my hands as I took a

sip, feeling more alert and focused on the letters I had

written down.

First, I examined the letters from the lighthouse.

M C H L G M Z S R N W T W L D L T N H G T

N T R H T D F F R N T M T S

Then I examined the vowels from the letter given to me

outside my razed apartment.

I A E O E I E I I E O I O I E E I E I E

I rested my hand on my face, staring at the cryptic

and strangely evocative letters. Whatever message they

held likely meant another trap.

"Okay, I've written everything down. Here are all the letters

from both the lighthouse and the letter," I said, showing my

Have You Seen Me? My Name is Claire Hines

notebook to Winters, who sat across from me. She held a plain white mug in her hands, the steam from her tea gracefully dancing.

"Interesting," she replied, copying the letters onto a larger sheet of paper.

"I'll give this to the commissioner," she said, leaving the room to hand him the paper.

"Where did you go?" I asked upon her return.

"I made a copy of your notes for Gomez. He'll distribute additional copies to the rest of the squad. The more eyes we have on this, the better," Winters declared.

I smiled at her as she studied my notes. "Where's your copy? Or are you planning to keep the original all to yourself?"

She looked up at me, playfully slapping my shoulder before focusing on my notebook. Watching her examine my notes made me realize that, despite my feelings for Claire, Winters was growing on me. In the short time we had spent together, I was beginning to like her.

Have You Seen Me? My Name is Claire Hines

"I think I've figured something out," she said, breaking the silence.

Our eyes locked, and without hesitation or warning, we kissed. It was different from the first time I kissed Claire. That kiss had felt somewhat staged, with her sister nearby, snapping a photo of us at the zoo. In jest, she had suggested a more romantic photo by capturing us in a kiss.

We obliged, but it didn't compare to this moment with Winters. I leaned back in my chair, taking a deep breath. Winters wore the same expression of shock and amazement.

"What just happened?" Winters asked, our eyes still locked.

"I'm not sure, but what did you figure out?" I asked, hoping to divert her attention from the awkwardness of the situation.

Gomez entered the room, eyeing us suspiciously. "Is something the matter? Am I interrupting something?"

"No, not at all," I quickly responded, hoping his suspicion wouldn't lead to any conclusions.

Have You Seen Me? My Name is Claire Hines

Clearing his throat, Gomez asked if we had made any

progress with the puzzle.

"Not yet," Winters answered.

"We're still working on it," I added.

"Well, someone else on the squad believes they've found

something," he declared. "You're not going to like this," he

reluctantly continued.

Winters and I looked at Gomez expectantly.

"What is it?" I asked.

"Officer Hill combined the vowels and letters together. The

first four letters and three vowels spell your name,

Michael," Gomez revealed.

"Why doesn't that surprise me?" I sarcastically remarked.

"There's more. The next two vowels and three letters spell

my name. But that's all we have so far. I hope you can

decipher the rest," Gomez explained.

Winters returned her focus to the paper, making notes.

"We will solve this," I reassured them both.

Have You Seen Me? My Name is Claire Hines

Chapter 23

The Puzzle – Part 2

"Gomez mentioned that the first set spells both my name and his. So that leaves us with the following set of letters."

S R N W T W L D L T N H G T N T R H T D F F

R N T M T S

"And the following set of vowels," I said to Winters.

I E I I E O I O I E E I E I E

"So, let's try writing this out," she said, tearing off the bottom half of the paper. She proceeded to write down the set of letters and vowels on the blank piece of paper.

"SIREN, WIT," Winters asked, combining the first few vowels and letters. "What does that mean?"

"Wait," I said, rearranging the same letters in a different order. "What if you write it like this: WIT? Wait, that can't be right."

"No, hold on, Michael," she said, pausing. "What if you... Oh, this is my name."

Have You Seen Me? My Name is Claire Hines

I looked at her and then at "Siren Wit."

"You're right! Just remove the extra letter 'I,' and it spells out 'Winters!'"

She frowned. "How does the person know who I am?"

"I don't know, but at least we're making progress."

It was challenging to approach this with a clear mind. Part of me felt guilty for allowing something to come between us.

"Okay, so the first set spells out your name, mine, and Gomez's. Let's figure the rest out. We now know that some of the letters are scrambled. Whoever wrote this is one clever maniac."

"You are a great detective," I said.

I stared at my notes, focusing on solving the puzzle rather than my attraction toward her. My eyes ran across the remaining set of letters and vowels:

W L D L T N H G T N T R H T D F F R N T M T S

I I E O I O I E E I E I E

WILDIL

I cupped my chin. *Focus Michael, what do you see?*

At the financial center where I work, it was always easy to read charts and figures, but nothing could prepare me for this. This was...

WILD.

"I wrote the word 'wild,' does that make any sense to you?" I asked Winters. She continued rearranging the letters to form different words, just as I was doing.

"They are scrambled, Michael. Try writing them out in a different order. Look, like this," she said, flipping the paper around to show me.

WILL.

"Okay, that makes more sense than 'Wild'," I said, feeling a sense of relief. However, frustration was still creeping in.

I examined what had been written so far:

Michael, Gomez, Winters will.

Then, I focused my attention on the remaining words and stared at them, trying to decipher their meaning.

Have You Seen Me? My Name is Claire Hines

D T N H G T N T R H T D F F R N T M T S

I E O I O I E E I E I E

"DIE TONIGHT," I said aloud with a mix of accomplishment and unease.

It was an unsettling feeling to realize that the message implied I would meet my demise tonight. Winters scrutinized what I had written, her expression mirroring a mix of concern and disbelief.

"That's correct. But wait, 'die tonight'?" Winters asked anxiously. "I should inform Gomez about this. Stay here and continue working on the rest of the puzzle."

I proceeded to jot down the remaining letters and vowels, determined to uncover more clues.

N T R H T D F F R N T M T S

O I E E I E I

Not hire fired.

Abruptly, my attention was diverted by the vibration of my phone. I glanced at the screen to find a text message from an unfamiliar phone number.

Have You Seen Me? My Name is Claire Hines

Did you figure it out yet? Time is running out.

The words sent a chilling sensation down my spine. While I wanted to wait for Winters' return, I couldn't keep the sender of this message waiting for a response.

Who the hell is this, and how did you get my number? I quickly typed, sending the message without hesitation. Moments ticked by as I anxiously stared at my phone, awaiting a reply.

Soon, a new message appeared:

There are more letters to be found,

Sit back and take a moment to look around.

Something blue will help reveal the rest,

Time is running out, so do your best.

I slid my phone back into my pocket and hastily left the meeting room. As I exited, I noticed an officer in a worn-out uniform. His appearance was distinct from the others at the station, bearing scars and wrinkles that hinted at a life filled with action. His white curly hair peeked out from beneath his low-worn police cap, concealing his eyes, which surveyed the surroundings like a predator hunting its prey.

Without saying a word, the officer walked away, catching my attention. I glimpsed at his name tag—Rellik. Suddenly, a realization struck me: Rellik spelled backward was "killer."

Bursting into Gomez's office, I interrupted their conversation. "I received a text from the kill..." I paused, comprehending the significance. "Wait a minute! He was here!"

Confused, Gomez inquired, "Who?"

"The officer standing outside the meeting room," I explained urgently.

Without wasting a moment, I turned and dashed out of the office. Winters' voice trailed behind me, calling my name, but my focus was on finding the truth. Exiting the police station, I found myself on an empty street, devoid of any sign of the mysterious officer.

Have You Seen Me? My Name is Claire Hines

Chapter 24

Rellik

I returned inside and noticed Gomez approaching me with his gun drawn.

"Did you see him?" he asked, reaching for his radio. "I'll instruct some officers to patrol the area."

The police station consisted of various offices, meeting rooms, a small kitchen, and a main area where the officers gathered. Below the station, there was a spacious garage housing the police vehicles and vans, as well as the kennel for the police dogs. On the second floor were the cells and a recreational center.

"Officer Anderson, review the security tapes. I want to know if this guy shows up, including timestamps and locations," Gomez commanded.

"Understood, sir," Anderson replied.

"Winters, examine Michael's phone. I need to trace the origin of the text messages," Gomez instructed.

"I'll do my best," she responded.

Have You Seen Me? My Name is Claire Hines

"He mentioned something about the meeting room. I'm going back to check it out," I stated.

"Logan, accompany Michael and assist him in inspecting the room," Gomez ordered.

Logan, a fellow officer of similar age, wore the standard police uniform.

"Let's get to it, Michael," Logan said, leading the way down the hallway and into the meeting room.

The motion sensor lights activated, but instead of the usual fluorescent light, a black light illuminated the room, exposing the ceiling adorned with letters and vowels.

"What the hell is all of this?" Logan exclaimed, sharing my disbelief.

Unlike the symbols at the lighthouse, these letters formed actual words. The lines were sharp and gave off a cryptic and menacing vibe.

"Well, it appears the puzzle has been solved," I declared.

I read the words aloud: "Fire, poison, knives, three will die tonight."

However, unlike before, the names of Gomez, Winters, and myself were absent.

Logan contacted Gomez over the radio, "Sir, you need to see this."

"Roger, on our way," Gomez responded.

Gomez entered the room accompanied by four other officers. They all stood frozen in shock as their eyes fell upon the chilling words.

"What in the hell..." Gomez trailed off, stunned. "Anderson, any updates on the security cameras?"

The walkie-talkie emitted a faint static sound.

"Negative, sir," Anderson's voice crackled through the walkie-talkie. "Unfortunately, the cameras have been disabled since last Wednesday."

"That's over a week!" Gomez exclaimed. "Why weren't we informed?"

Anderson remained silent.

"Winters, please tell me you have good news about the cellphone location," Gomez pleaded.

"Negative, sir. The sender has managed to evade our tracking," Winters replied.

"Dammit!" Gomez shouted, slamming his fist on the conference table in frustration.

"This guy is skilled, incredibly skilled," Logan remarked.

Gomez grunted angrily and stormed out of the room.

"Is he going to be okay?" I asked, concerned.

Locking eyes with me, Logan nodded. "Yeah, give him a few hours. He'll head back to his office for a drink or two. I haven't seen him this upset since Winters accidentally crashed into his prized 1967 Chevy Camaro."

Just as Winters entered the meeting room and saw the words, I recounted what had transpired with Gomez. "Well, one thing's certain, according to the puzzle, three people are going to die tonight. Unfortunately, those three people are us," Winters solemnly stated.

Have You Seen Me? My Name is Claire Hines

Chapter 25

The Diner

"Gomez?" Winters knocked on his office door.

The drawn window shades prevented us from seeing inside. According to Winters, this usually meant one of two things: Gomez was engrossed in researching a challenging case, like Claire's disappearance, or he was indulging in his favorite bottle of Johnny Walker Blue whiskey.

"What can I say, the man has expensive taste," Winters remarked.

We were both concerned about Gomez, especially since he had seen his name on the list of people marked for death.

"Comish," Winters added, "We're going to grab some dinner and then head back to my place. Logan will join us."

"Fine, fine," Gomez was still feeling disgruntled, yelled from behind his office door.

Have You Seen Me? My Name is Claire Hines

It remained firmly locked, a clear indication that he didn't want to be disturbed. However, given the circumstances, Winters chose to ignore it.

We left the station and drove to Lou's Diner in Bridgeport, aiming to lay low and increase our chances of survival. Winters worried about Gomez being alone in his locked office, but I reassured her that it was for his own safety. The ringing bell announced our entrance, grabbing the attention of everyone inside.

"Why is the floor sticky?" Logan asked bluntly.

His question went unanswered as he settled into a worn vinyl booth. The chairs had seen better days. I sat across from Logan, and Winters sat beside me, maintaining a certain distance. She didn't want Logan to notice the unexpected attraction between us.

"So, what can I get you kids?" the waitress asked.

Gomez sat in his office, taking a sip from his whiskey glass. The amber liquid caressed his lips gently, providing some much-needed relief. His phone rang.

Have You Seen Me? My Name is Claire Hines

"This is Gomez," he answered, speaking into the receiver.

"Commissioner, I have the results from the hair sample. You won't believe whose hair it belongs to," the lab technician informed him.

"Who?" Gomez inquired.

"It's matching someone we know. But there's more."

"Go on," Gomez urged.

The lab technician paused briefly. "We found another strand of hair accidentally, inside Michael's apartment on the night of the explosion. Both strands of hair belong to Michael."

The square glass nearly slipped from Gomez's hands when he heard Michael's name.

The waitress smiled at us, her blue eyeshadow heavily applied, and her lips glistening with pink lipstick. It was unclear whether she was trying to attract or scare the customers.

"What's the special of the day?" Logan asked the waitress, whose nametag read Mitch.

"Ham hocks," she grumbled.

Have You Seen Me? My Name is Claire Hines

"I have no idea what that is, but I'm feeling adventurous tonight! Mitch, bring me an order of that!" Logan exclaimed playfully.

"I'll have the spaghetti with meat sauce," I said, opting not to inquire further about the mysterious meat sauce.

Mitch raised her eyebrow and jotted down my order.

"Winters?" Mitch asked with a dry, raspy voice that reflected years of cigarettes and sadness. "The usual?"

Winters looked up from the menu and nodded eagerly.

"One double cheeseburger with onion rings and a strawberry milkshake, got it."

Winters smiled with anticipation.

Mitch shrugged and walked away, leaving behind a trail of stale department store perfume.

Before I could say anything, Logan interrupted. "Really? You're ordering a meal fit for a teenager? Aren't you a little too old for that?"

I looked at Logan in shock. It was a rude remark.

"Hey, now, let her eat whatever she wants. Remember, we're supposed to die tonight," I retorted sarcastically.

Have You Seen Me? My Name is Claire Hines

Winters looked at me and playfully punched my arm, eliciting a loud "Ow!" from me.

"Speak for yourself, Mikey. I'm not dying tonight. And even if I do, at least my last meal will be my favorite!" Winters declared, slamming her fist on the table.

The clattering of dishes and glasses resonated through the diner, but the few patrons paid no attention. We laughed together, a momentary respite from the weight of the message we had received.

"Dying tonight," the thought lingered in the back of my mind.

Am I going to die tonight?

Chapter 26

First One

"Sergeant Decker, we haven't heard from Gomez in a few hours. He has been locked up in his office," reported Anderson.

The blinds were drawn, and the door remained locked. Both officers grew concerned, sensing that something was amiss. Normally, after a few hours, Gomez would step out for a cigarette or engage in shop talk with Decker.

Decker gently knocked on the door. "Sir, are you in there?"

Anderson looked at Decker and shook his head. Decker remained calm, assuming that Gomez was passed out from excessive drinking.

"Don't worry about it, Decker. Let him be," suggested Anderson, stepping away from the door. However, Decker didn't budge.

Ignoring Anderson's advice, Decker attempted to pick the lock. "Leave him alone! You'll only upset Gomez!"

Have You Seen Me? My Name is Claire Hines

After failing to pick the lock successfully, Decker sighed and gave up. Both officers walked away from the office, while their colleagues returned to their desks and resumed their duties.

Decker sat at his desk, his attention still fixed on the commissioner's office. The silence was unsettling, and he knew that something was awry. Hours passed, and Gomez remained locked in his office, defying his usual schedule of leaving.

Both Anderson and Decker, aware of Gomez's methodical nature, anticipated his emergence from the office, either flustered or hurriedly rushing home to his family.

Anderson looked up from his computer and decided it was his turn to check on the commissioner. He gently knocked on the office door. Decker joined him, stating, "Okay, something is definitely wrong. He should be coming out of his office now."

Have You Seen Me? My Name is Claire Hines

Decker instructed Anderson to retrieve a crowbar from the storage room to force the door open. Moments later, Anderson returned with the crowbar, and they pried the door open. Detectives, officers, and janitorial staff watched as the office door swung open.

Inside, Gomez lay unconscious on his desk. A partially filled bottle of amber-colored alcohol had tipped over, staining his white uniform and the papers strewn across the desk.

"See? Nothing's wrong. He's just passed out drunk," Decker declared, scoffing in disgust at Gomez and the embarrassing scene.

Ignoring Decker's comment, Anderson approached Gomez to inspect and confirm his well-being. He gently touched the commissioner's right arm through his thin white shirt, only to be met with an icy coldness. "Something's wrong," Anderson declared, resting his fingers on Gomez's neck. His voice quivered with profound sadness. "There's no pulse. He's gone."

Have You Seen Me? My Name is Claire Hines

The room filled with sounds of grief and remorse. Decker, attempting to alleviate the pain of everyone witnessing the sight, exclaimed, "We need to get the forensic team here now!"

"Step aside, officer. This is now an official crime scene. We need to determine what happened!" Anderson proclaimed. The forensics team arrived and began examining the commissioner's desk for evidence of foul play.

"Have the medical staff test the blood and alcohol. This doesn't appear to be an accident," instructed one of the officers.

"Wait, what's that?" Decker noticed something protruding from the front pocket of Gomez's shirt. The forensics team member retrieved the item and read aloud the note it contained.

"Now the mouse takes the cheese,

Poisoned and killed by his own disease.

The first of two has been taken away,

Two remain that will die today."

Have You Seen Me? My Name is Claire Hines

Decker was shocked by the words. "Get on the phone and contact Winters! She's with Michael and Logan. They're all in danger!"

Anderson left the room and called Winters. It wouldn't be easy to break the news of Gomez's death to her, as he was like a father figure to her. Anderson selected her name on his phone and dialed the number. "Winters? Are you sitting down? There's something I need to tell you."

Chapter 27

The Phone Call

"What is it, Anderson?" Winters inquired, and Logan and I watched with anticipation.

I could sense that the caller had devastating news to deliver. Winters' brown eyes met mine as she listened to the voice on the other end.

"What do you mean? He what? Are you sure?" Winters covered her mouth, her eyes brimming with sadness.

"Oh my... yes... I understand. Okay, we're on our way there now," Winters said, tossing her phone onto the table before breaking down.

"What happened? Are you okay?" Logan asked. I placed my hands on Winters' shoulders as she covered her face.

She looked at me, and without hesitation, she fell into my chest, sobbing heavily. Her tears soaked my shirt, leaving me at a loss for words because I didn't know what had occurred.

"Well, spill it. Who was that on the phone?" Logan demanded.

"We need to leave!" Winters exclaimed, abruptly pulling away from me.

"Michael, take the keys to my apartment. We'll meet you there," she instructed.

"What happened? Tell me!" I demanded, feeling frustration build up within me due to the lack of information.

Winters glanced at Logan, then back at me. "He's gone."

"Who's gone?" Logan asked.

"Gomez. They found him... he..." Winters stammered. "I don't know what happened, okay? Anderson told me we need to return to the station immediately."

Logan tossed a wrinkled fifty-dollar bill onto the table. "Tell our charming waitress to keep the change, okay, Michael?" They headed toward the exit, and Winters turned to look at me.

"Michael, go to my apartment. Wait for my call. We will come back. I will come back, Michael, I..."

Have You Seen Me? My Name is Claire Hines

"I understand," I interrupted before she could finish her sentence. "I'll wait for you and your phone call."

She gave a brief smile, then left the diner. Mitch hurriedly approached our table, a scowl on her face, as if she thought we were going to leave without paying the bill.

"Leaving so soon?"

Ignoring her question, I handed her the money.

"Keep the change," I declared.

I grabbed my coat and made my way toward the exit. Suddenly, a massive explosion ripped through the night air as Logan started the car. Before I could fully step out, the force of the blast knocked me back.

The front windows shattered, and Venetian blinds fell from their places, littering the vacant booths. Shards of glass rained down on me as I fell, hitting the decorative ceramic floor hard. Amidst the chaos, I heard the cries of patrons and staff, including Mitch's raspy yell.

"It's a terrorist attack!" Someone shouted, fleeing into the kitchen.

Have You Seen Me? My Name is Claire Hines

As I crawled, my hands scraped against the glass shards, and my vision blurred from the impact. A man walked into the diner, his footsteps crunching on the broken glass. He stood over me, scanning the room as if searching for someone, then swiftly pulled out a large assault rifle from beneath his black trench coat.

"Oh no! Run!" another patron yelled as the man fired several shots into the air.

Empty bullet casings fell on me as I scrambled toward a nearby vacant booth, feeling trapped. Fear urged me to run, but instinct made me stay put. In this position, I could feign being dead. The thunderous sound of the gun deafened me, and the man wore a chilling smile as he continued shooting.

It was Mammon, the same man who had haunted me from the beginning, and likely responsible for the deaths of everyone, including Winters. This monster had destroyed my apartment and kidnapped my fiancée, turning my life into a living nightmare.

He emptied the rifle's clip, discarding it on the floor before reloading. More shots rang out until the diner fell silent, devoid of screams.

The man's gaze met mine as he aimed the weapon in my direction. Anticipating my end, I closed my eyes tightly, ready to embrace death and join Winters, Crosby, Frank, and perhaps even Claire.

Thoughts of everyone I had known and lost raced through my mind, making my heart pound. My trembling hands covered my face, fearing the imminent gunshot. The clicking sound of an empty assault rifle reassured me that, for now, I was safe.

"Aw, looks like I'm all out of ammo," the man declared, erupting into hysterical laughter. "It's time to go, Michael."

He discarded the empty rifle as if it were a mere toy, causing glass and debris to crunch beneath his feet as he approached. Grabbing me, he covered my face with a damp, white rag. The odor of stale metallic drugs invaded my nostrils. I became limp as he effortlessly slung my body over his shoulder, resembling a discarded ragdoll. Through

Have You Seen Me? My Name is Claire Hines

my fading vision, I glimpsed the lifeless bodies, including Mitch, lying in pools of blood. Mitch's tear-filled eyes met mine, lips quivering but silent, aware that any sound could mean certain death.

I felt a pang of guilt for the negative thoughts I had earlier about her. The drug took hold, clouding my vision until darkness consumed me. I was losing consciousness. Crackling fire nearby indicated we had passed the remnants of where Logan and Winters had been killed.

Chapter 28

Trapped

I found myself walking through a forest, birds chirping overhead. Mist hung over the shrubbery, and flowers bloomed through the haze. It was a peaceful moment, a rarity in our busy lives. As I walked, I felt a sense of weightlessness and wondered if this was where I truly belonged, a break from reality.

Suddenly, the clanging of metal tools snapped me back to the present. Opening my eyes, I found myself in a dimly lit room, my hands tightly bound. Mammon stood before me, arranging tools on a surgical tray. The room was empty except for the two of us and a covered figure beside me, evoking a sense of death.

A crimson-colored bulb buzzed overhead, encased in a protective cage. The bare concrete walls and steel door gave the room an eerie atmosphere. I realized I had no idea how long I had been there or where exactly I was.

Have You Seen Me? My Name is Claire Hines

Mammon turned to face me, gripping my hair with a rubber-gloved hand. His appearance had changed since our last encounter, with combed-back greasy hair and a nurse's uniform. I asked him who he was, and he seemed surprised by my question.

After releasing his grip, Mammon revealed his identity as Gomez, my nurse. Confused, I mentioned the hospital, but he dismissed it as one of my episodes. I insisted on knowing where Claire was, and he revealed the person beside me to be a doll resembling her.

Refusing to accept his story, I accused him of kidnapping Claire after shooting me. He denied it, claiming I was mistaken and needed to remember what truly happened. Before summoning "Doctor Winters" for help, he prepared a syringe and injected me, saying it would jog my memory.

As the red lights flickered and the buzzing sound grew deafening, I closed my eyes tightly. When I opened them, I found myself bound to a hospital bed in a different room.

Have You Seen Me? My Name is Claire Hines

Chapter 29

Sunnyside Sanitorium

The doctor, named Winters according to her nametag, entered the room wearing a white lab coat. She was an attractive woman who resembled the Winters I had encountered at the police station, but her demeanor was less affectionate towards me.

"Hello there, Michael. How are we feeling today?" she asked.

"Confused. I need to get out of here and find Claire!" I yelled in frustration.

Winters shook her head and pointed towards the chair beside me. "Claire is right there, see?" she gestured. I looked and saw a doll with red hair and green eyes, dressed in a red dress. She reminded me of how Claire looked the night she was taken from me.

"I don't understand. Why are you pointing at this doll?" I questioned.

Have You Seen Me? My Name is Claire Hines

"Because this is Claire. You use this doll as a way to cope. Don't you remember what happened to you?" Winters explained.

"I... I... she... was... taken..." I struggled to find the words.

The doctor shook her head again. "No, she was not taken from you. Nobody was kidnapped." She turned to the nurse. "Did you administer lorazepam, clonazepam, or diazepam?"

"Yes, I gave him a full dose of lorazepam," Gomez, the nurse, replied.

"Michael, look at me," Winters said, shining a bright flashlight into my eyes. "He is slowly coming back to us. Let me help you remember, Michael."

"I saw you die. The explosion at the diner. Mammon," I recalled.

The doctor shook her head once more. "Mammon? You mean the demon of greed? That's a manifestation from your imagination, a result of the trauma you experienced. Think back, Michael. Do you remember the night at the diner? What was the name of the diner?" She checked her medical records.

"Lou's Diner," we said simultaneously.

"Good, you remember! We're making progress. Now, do you remember why you went to the diner?" she inquired.

"Yes, you wanted to eat there," I replied.

The doctor sighed. "No, let's go further back. Do you remember your full name?"

"My full name?" I questioned, trying to recall. But I couldn't remember my last name. "I... don't remember my last name."

She smiled warmly. "It's okay, Michael. I'll help you remember. Your name is Michael Fisher."

"Michael Fisher?" I repeated. "But then that means... the money."

"Yes, your money. You lost everything and blamed your financial advisor. You began stalking him and discovered that he frequented Lou's Diner once a week. Do you remember what happened?" Winters explained.

"The diner?" I shook my head, unable to recall.

Have You Seen Me? My Name is Claire Hines

"You sought revenge. You walked into the diner and shot everyone inside. Then you blamed this..." Winters checked her notes. "...Mammon," she stated.

"Yes! Mammon! He's the reason for all this!" I exclaimed.

"No, Michael. This was your doing. Your greed led to your downfall. You created this story about your fiancée being kidnapped. But in reality, the police found you at the diner. You killed everyone inside. They shot at you multiple times, but you miraculously survived and woke up in a hospital," the doctor revealed.

I stared at them in disbelief.

"But what about the power plants? The explosions? Crosby, Muller, Frank, Parker, Naminski, Logan... they were all killed. Officer Decker and Anderson, we were together at the station, solving the riddles," I questioned.

"Crosby, Muller, Frank, Parker, and Amanda were the names of the officers and FBI agents who shot and arrested you at the diner. Parker Naminski was your lawyer. Decker Anderson was the judge in your case. Your father worked at the power plant. Crawford was the name

Have You Seen Me? My Name is Claire Hines

of the station. You lived in an apartment building managed by a Lithuanian family. Unfortunately, you blew up that building the same evening as the diner shooting, trying to cover your tracks. Everything else, like the train and the lighthouse by the lake, was a product of your imagination based on past experiences," Winters explained.

"What about the riddles?" I asked.

"The riddles?" Winters checked her notes as Gomez handed her several folded pieces of paper. "Oh, right! The letters. Yes, you wrote those yourself. This Mammon persona you created was a way for you to escape from reality. But the truth is, Michael, this is what you've done. The trauma you experienced made you forget that it was real. Instead, your mind created this fictional world where your fiancée was kidnapped, and you needed to help the police find her. Every time we talk, you bring up finding her. It's only through conversations like this and administering drugs to calm your mind that you remember who you truly are."

"I... did this?" I said, stunned by the revelation.

Have You Seen Me? My Name is Claire Hines

"Yes. You claimed insanity as part of your plea bargain. That's why you're here under our care," Winters confirmed.

"Where is here?" I asked, confused.

"Sunnyside Sanitorium. This is your home now. We'll make sure you receive the care you need. Now get some rest."

After the doctor and nurse left the room, I lay quietly and stared at the ceiling. It seemed the riddles were true after all. I had died and awakened in this place.

www.ingramcontent.com/pod-product-compliance
Lightning Source LLC
Chambersburg PA
CBHW061236170626
46809CB00007B/2704